SCHOOL of SECRETS

DESCENDANTS

SCHOOL of SECRETS

CJ'S TREASURE CHASE

Jessica Brody

DISNEY PRESS

Los Angeles • New York

Printed in the United States of America
First Hardcover Edition, August 2016
3 5 7 9 10 8 6 4 2
FAC-020093-16308

Library of Congress Control Number: 2016939519
ISBN 978-1-4847-7864-7

For more Disney Press fun, visit www.disneybooks.com
Visit DisneyDescendants.com

THIS LABEL APPLIES TO TEXT STOCK

MORE NEW BOOKS COMING SOON IN
THE SCHOOL OF SECRETS SERIES . . .

NEXT:
FREDDIE'S SHADOW CARDS

MAROONED

The girl was a child of the Isle of the Lost. You know the one. Just off the coast of the United States of Auradon. The isle was home to every evil villain and sidekick who had ever plotted, cursed, cheated, plundered, or wreaked havoc.

The girl was seven, and although she had been marooned there when she was a baby, she always knew she was destined for greater things. Far-off places and grand adventures. Storming seas and buried treasures. Especially buried treasures . . .

One night, after the hanging oil lanterns had burned out, the little girl crept through the dark ship she called home to sneak into her father's study. Most of his belongings had been confiscated after he was exiled to the Isle of the Lost, but just under the old ship wheel sat a large wooden treasure chest with a rusty gold clasp, concealed by a dusty white sheet.

The girl was sure there had been a time when the treasure chest was overflowing with diamonds, rubies, sapphires, and pearls as white as the foam of crashing waves.

Now the wood was old, peeling, splintered. The hinges creaked when she lifted the lid. In the moonlight that shone through the porthole, she peered at the item hidden deep inside.

It was a map.

The girl lifted it and touched the yellowed paper, with its crisp brown edges and faded ink. The map was incomplete. The finely drawn details started at the bottom left corner of the aged paper, depicting a compass, waves of an ocean, a forgotten island, and the beginnings of a dotted trail. Then the map just stopped. Maybe it was the girl's keen intuition, a trait passed down to her by her shrewd and cunning father. Or maybe it was hope. But the girl had a feeling that the map was magical. That was what lured her back to look at it night after night.

The girl believed that given the opportunity, the map would cease to be just a piece of a paper and turn into something else. Something greater. She considered the possibilities. Maybe it led to an all-powerful treasure. Maybe someone had enchanted the rest of the map to disappear . . . only to reappear in the right place at the right time to the right person.

She traced the dotted trail with her fingertip until it vanished into nothing. She ran her hand over the empty space that she dreamed held the promise of adventure, wondering if the rest of the map would ever be revealed to her.

Magic was banned on the Isle of the Lost. King Beast had made sure of it. The girl knew that. But she also knew that magic did exist someplace else: Auradon. The girl spent that night, like every night, dreaming about finally stealing the map and taking it there, activating its magic, and using it to find the greatest pirate's treasure ever known. . . .

As she placed the map back in the chest and closed the lid, she whispered into the darkness, "Someday."

Oh, how time flies.

AHOY . . . AND STUFF

Hi. I'm CJ, the teenage daughter of Captain Hook.

You may think that as the descendant of a villainous pirate, I'm all "plunder" this and "pillage" that. And you wouldn't be entirely wrong. But what I am, more than anything, is an adventurer. That's definitely something I get from my once-upon-a-time-swashbuckling dad. But enough about him. This story is about me.

The problem is it's pretty hard to have an adventure when you're trapped on the Isle of the Lost with no way out. And for a while there, I was convinced that I was as stuck as a barnacle on a boat. But then something unexpected happened.

I was magically transported to Auradon Prep through Jordan's genie lamp.

I won't get into all the details . . . blah, blah, blah, magic lamp, three wishes, whatever. One minute I was hanging out on the Isle of the Lost with my best friend, Freddie, minding my own business, and the next minute, Freddie and I both disappeared in a puff of pink smoke and were magically transported to Auradon Prep!

As soon as we got there, I hid. Freddie, on the other hand, was more than happy to make her presence known. Freddie, I should mention, is very persuasive—something she got from her dad, the evil and awesome Dr. Facilier. One of Freddie's secret weapons is her "velvet voice," which is so smooth and mesmerizing, it gets her exactly what she wants. It's like vocal black magic. She managed to convince King Ben (the son of that beast who locked us all away on the Isle of the Lost) to let her stay at Auradon Prep as a student. She even got her own dorm room.

And you know what that means, don't you?

I, CJ Hook, am now her roommate.

Well, her secret stowaway roommate.

But it doesn't matter. I don't plan on hanging around here for very long. I have big plans now that I'm finally in Auradon—<u>very</u> big plans.

Let the pirate games begin. . . .

STOWAWAY

*So I finally got off the Isle of
the Lost and into Auradon!*

*But it turns out hiding in Freddie's room is worse
than being stuffed into Davy Jones's locker.
(I hear that place is cramped.)*

"So why exactly are you stowing away in my room?"
Freddie asked CJ.

They were settling into Freddie's new Auradon Prep
dorm room, which fortunately had two beds. CJ would
need a place to sleep while she enacted her big plan. She'd
also need some food to eat and maybe a sink to wash her
face in—although pirates were known for going months
without bathing. (The past year, CJ had gotten her

father, Captain Hook, a bottle of Rotting Kelp cologne for his birthday, to remind him of his glory days on the high seas.)

CJ glared at one of the beds, as if she were staring down an incoming enemy ship. It was pink and covered in ruffles. CJ didn't mind ruffles, as long as they were white and on her shirt. *Not* on her bed. "Blimey. This just won't fly."

"CJ," Freddie prompted, "do you have a plan or something?"

CJ pulled off the blanket, ripped the ruffles from the hem, and flung the blanket across the four posters of the bed, fashioning it into a makeshift sail. Then she grabbed a black marker from the nearby desk and drew a skull and crossbones on the pillowcase. She took a step back to examine her work. "Better," she said.

Freddie placed her hands on her hips and frowned. She was wearing a pin-striped red-and-purple dress, white-and-black ankle boots, and a tiny purple top hat, which sat slightly crooked atop her long, shiny black hair. "Please tell me you aren't just going to crash here and play a bunch of pranks on people."

CJ collapsed onto her newly transformed bed and flashed Freddie one of her signature mischievous grins, complete with a wink. She was really good at those. Freddie might have had the "velvet voice" market cornered, but CJ could smirk her way out of any plank walk.

CJ was just counting the minutes until Freddie would leave and she could finally be alone. But she couldn't tell Freddie that. If Freddie knew what CJ was really up to, she might want to help. And CJ didn't need help. Not even from her best friend.

"CJ," Freddie said warningly.

CJ glanced around the room, her smirk quickly morphing into a disapproving scowl. "Eew. The decoration in this place is truly disgusting. I mean, it looks like a fairy threw up in here."

Freddie walked to CJ's bed and sat down next to her. "Stop changing the subject."

CJ yawned, kicked off her crocodile-skin boots, and fell onto her back, her red pirate coat flaring out around her like wings. "What was the subject again?"

Freddie threw up her hands. "What are we doing here?"

"*You*," CJ said, sitting up to face her friend, "are going to school to learn about kindness and decency and the chemical compound of fairy dust." The sarcasm was thick in her voice. Freddie shuddered.

It was clear from the look on Freddie's face that she hadn't quite thought this whole student thing through yet. "And you?" she asked CJ.

CJ reached out and touched her friend's nose. "Don't you worry your pretty little shrunken head about me."

Freddie didn't look convinced. "Whenever you say that is when I worry the *most* about you."

CJ just flashed her the smirk again. Then, for the tenth time since they'd magically arrived in Auradon, CJ reached into the pocket of her coat and ran her finger-tips over the very special object she'd been keeping with her since she was a little girl. Fortunately, it had survived the trip. Her whole secret plan depended on it.

Freddie sighed in surrender and stood up. "Well, maybe they'll have a music class I can take or something. Singing will be a good distraction from whatever horrors Headmistress Fairy Godmother has in store for me." She turned back to CJ and pouted. "Whatever it is you're planning, can you at least *try* not to get caught? The last time you plotted secretly, you got us both in huge trouble."

CJ shook her head. "Two minutes in Auradon and you've already gone soft on me? Since when do *you* care about getting in trouble?"

Freddie seemed to think about that for a second. "I just . . ." She hesitated. "I don't want to get kicked out of this place before we've had a chance to do some real damage, you know?"

But CJ wasn't at all convinced by her explanation. Freddie's usual mischievous spirit wasn't in it. She sounded almost worried. And Freddie *never* sounded worried. When you're the daughter of the great and powerful Dr. Facilier, a man who can turn another grown man into a frog, you have very little to worry about.

CJ wondered if Freddie was already starting to like it there, which was *not* acceptable.

What if Freddie ended up wanting to stay? Like for*ever*?

Maybe CJ was just paranoid after what had happened with Mal and Evie, but she didn't want to lose *another* friend to this pixie palace.

Not that she had time to worry about that. The clock was ticking and she had work to do. Plus, she *hated* ticking clocks.

Some things are just hereditary.

ARRRR!

*Alone at last. And not
a second too soon!*

Something's been burning a hole in my pocket.

Freddie left for lunch at the banquet hall and CJ was finally alone.

She knew that was her big chance.

This is what I've been waiting for ever since I was a little girl, she thought as she reached into the pocket of her red pirate coat and pulled out the cracked and yellowed scroll of paper she'd been itching to look at ever since they'd arrived in Auradon.

She carried it to the white dresser next to the door. With a quiver in her heart and a thumping in the pit of her stomach, she ever so carefully began to unfurl the page, revealing her beloved treasure map.

As a child she had spent many nights gazing at the scuffed paper, with its crispy edges and worn black ink. She had wasted many hours tracing her fingertip along the dotted line that had simply stopped at the barrier surrounding the island she'd called home. She had dreamed of the moment when she would finally arrive in Auradon, a place where magic wasn't forbidden, and the map would be complete.

Now that moment had arrived.

With trembling fingers, she finished unrolling the paper, and a tiny gasp escaped her lips.

It had happened. It was real.

The map had *changed*.

Even though she had predicted it, even though she had been waiting for that moment for as long as she could remember, she jumped away from the dresser in shock, as though afraid the map might attack her.

Then, of course, she immediately rushed back to study the wondrous transformation.

There were so many new, unfamiliar things on the page she didn't even know where to look first. Fields and trees and oceans. Buildings and towns and castles.

The kingdom of Auradon—with its curvy borders and harbors—had seemingly appeared out of nowhere.

With excitement pumping through her pirate veins, CJ noticed that the dotted trail—the one she had traced over and over with her tiny fingers years earlier—had expanded, too. It had grown and now traveled, from the desolate, magic-forsaken island, across the sea, over the land, to the city of Auradon.

For the first time in as long as she could remember, CJ felt giddy. She felt hopeful.

She felt *happy*.

She followed the newly extended trail with her fingertip, knowing it was leading her straight to the treasure she'd spent her entire life dreaming about.

She knew it would be big. Riches beyond her wildest dreams. After all, it was her father, the once-great Captain Hook, who had kept the map hidden all those years. He wouldn't have wasted his time unless there was something worthwhile waiting at the end.

Of course, he probably hadn't expected the map to be stolen by his own daughter. But could he really blame her? He had taught her well.

The treasure would surely be enough to buy CJ a ship of her very own—one with great big sails and a gold skull decorating the hull. And, of course, a plank for her many prisoners to walk.

Once she had her ship, she would be free. Forever.

But something was wrong. She stared at the map, turning it this way and that. All those years, she had been sure the map would be complete once she'd found her way off the Isle of the Lost. She had sworn it would lead her right to the treasure. But it was not complete. Far from it. Although a multitude of new things had been revealed, the page was still over half empty.

CJ could see the great ocean that separated the Isle of the Lost from the kingdom of Auradon. She could see Auradon City on the coast, Belle's Harbor to the west, and Belle and Beast's castle to the north. But that was it. Only a small part of the map had been revealed since she'd arrived in Auradon. The rest of it was still missing.

She tried everything she could think of—tapping it, shaking it, rerolling and unrolling it—but nothing worked. The map stayed as it was: incomplete, unfinished.

CJ wondered if something had gone wrong, if maybe some of the enchantment had worn off after years of being banished to a place where magic was not only forbidden but impossible.

She started to feel panicky. She started to pace and fidget and *growl*. She was close to crumpling up the useless map and tossing it out the window.

But then, during her relentless scowling and pacing, she noticed something.

Words.

Written in swirling cursive penmanship.

She hadn't noticed them before because she had been too distracted by the brand-new section of the map. The words were scrawled alongside the dotted trail.

She bent forward, twirling a beaded strand of her wild golden-brown hair between her thumb and forefinger. As she read the words, her heart started to pound again.

In this historic site of the learned
Lies a special stone unturned.
Find it among the tulips so bold
And your future will shine bright with gold.

CJ slapped herself on the forehead.

Of course! she thought. Treasure maps were never *easy* to follow. Otherwise everyone would find the gold.

Treasure maps were like pirates—shrewd and sly and mischievous.

It was a clue!

A clue that would lead her to the loot!

She just had to be clever enough to follow it.

And CJ was as clever as they came.

One day she would be as great a pirate as her father once had been. Maybe even better! CJ had listened to Captain Hook's stories for years, and she had learned from them. She knew better than to surrender to flying boys in green tights or be tricked by repulsive fairies.

She would prove herself worthy of the great name Hook. She would follow the clue wherever it led. She would find the treasure and get her pirate ship so her life's adventure could finally begin.

CJ reread the clue, feeling extremely confident.

A historic site of the learned?

That was kind of obvious. The clue was clearly referring to Auradon Prep. And she was already there! Now all she had to do was find the stone unturned in the tulips so bold and she would be well on her way to riches.

Smiling, CJ rolled up the map and returned it to her

pocket. She was already plotting, formulating a foolproof plan.

If she was going to find this special stone, she would have to do some serious reconnaissance work—familiarize herself with the territory, listen in on people's conversations, gather information.

Explore.

"Blast! I wish I had a compass," CJ muttered to herself. She knew it would make her quest much easier. But the sad fact was she'd never owned a compass. It was a great travesty for a pirate to be without one. Like a fairy godmother without a wand.

Her father used to have one—a very special one. He talked about it all the time back on the Isle of the Lost. How it was made from solid gold with a single flawless diamond in the center. How the diamond alone was worth more money than CJ could ever imagine.

Then he would angrily recount the story of how King Beast's men took it when he was banished to the island, the same way they took away Maleficent's scepter and Dr. Facilier's voodoo talisman and the magic from every mirror in Evil Queen's house.

That beautiful gold compass had been Captain Hook's source of strength and confidence. Without it, he was just a shell of the great sea captain he used to be. And King Beast knew that.

So, of course, compasses were a sore spot among the Hooks. It was nearly impossible to navigate without one, and CJ was wondering how she was going to manage it.

She creaked open the door to the hallway and poked her head outside, listening for footsteps. Everyone seemed to be at lunch.

Her stomach growled angrily at the thought of food. CJ rolled her eyes. How was she supposed to be stealth when her body was making sounds like that?

Apparently, before she could start her epic hunt for buried treasure, she was going to have to search for something to eat.

So inconvenient.

KEEP A SHARP LOOKOUT!

Time to explore this princess place.

*I can't believe Mal and Evie
actually **LIKE** it here.*

CJ soon discovered that sneaking around Auradon Prep was a breeze.

It was nothing like trying to sneak around the Isle of the Lost, where everyone was suspicious and paranoid. At Auradon Prep, people were *trusting*.

People were chumps.

And CJ knew it was always easier to take advantage of chumps.

She crept through the halls like a red-coated ghost

and no one even took notice. She stole food right out from under their noses and no one even batted an eye. And it wasn't exactly like she was being super stealth about any of this stuff, either. The people there were just that naive.

CJ spent the next few days crawling under tables and hiding behind corners, listening in on people's conversations. But she was quickly becoming bored by the lack of interesting conversation around the place. And she had yet to hear anything that would help her find a stone unturned.

One afternoon, however, she was convinced she'd caught her first break when she was hiding in the bushes outside one of the dorm room windows and she heard someone say the word *tulip*.

Find it among the tulips so bold . . .

CJ immediately perked up and she eased herself closer to the window.

"Oh, tulips would be divine!" said a girl with a British accent. CJ immediately recognized the voice as Ally's. She'd learned over the past few days that Ally was the daughter of Alice, who had fallen down a rabbit hole and ended up in a place called Wonderland.

"No. It *has* to be roses," someone with a snooty voice

said. It was definitely Audrey, the daughter of Princess Aurora.

CJ snuck right up to the window so she could peer through the sheer curtains. Inside the dorm room sat Ally, Audrey, Freddie, Mal, Evie, Jordan, and Jane, the daughter of Headmistress Fairy Godmother.

"Every ball should have roses," Audrey went on, smoothing out her poofy pink dress.

CJ rolled her eyes and stifled a frustrated sigh. She should have known they were talking about the upcoming Neon Lights Ball. It was all anyone seemed to care about around that place. Sneaking around Auradon Prep, CJ had quickly discovered that princesses were obsessed with two things: parties and what they would wear to parties.

"I prefer thorns," Mal said, crossing her arms over her purple leather jacket.

"Or apples," Evie suggested optimistically. She was dressed in her signature deep blue with hints of red.

"An apple is *not* a flower," Audrey argued. "The ballroom *has* to be decorated with *flowers*. Not fruit."

"Says who?" Evie retorted, challenging her.

Audrey huffed. "Says *everyone*!"

"I don't know," Jane said meekly. She had wide eyes,

auburn hair, and a sickeningly sweet smile. "We *could* decorate with pumpkins."

"No," Audrey said. "No vegetables."

Crawling crabs, she's bossy, CJ thought.

"Technically a pumpkin is a gourd, which makes it a fruit," Evie pointed out.

"Anyway!" Princess Bossypants went on. "Let's talk about music."

Freddie, who had previously seemed uninterested in the conversation, suddenly sat up straighter. "Oh! Actually, I've been thinking about the music. I thought maybe I could sing. I've been learning to play guitar and—"

"That's okay," Audrey said, cutting her off. "Lonnie is going to handle the music. She's a DJ. We just have to pick our theme song."

"Fine. Whatever," Freddie mumbled, and slumped in her chair. CJ immediately felt angry. How dare Audrey shoot down her friend like that! The girl needed to be taught a serious lesson.

So later, after everyone in the building had gone to sleep, CJ snuck into the art studio, grabbed a tube of super-stick glue, and crept into the kitchens. She quickly found what she was looking for in one of the freezers and headed for the student lockers outside. Because everyone there was so trusting, the lockers didn't even have locks on them, which made CJ's job much easier.

They should call them un*lockers,* CJ thought with a smirk as she hid her little "gift" inside Audrey's locker and then spread a thick layer of glue around the edge of the door.

She eased the door shut and gave it a firm push.

Satisfied with her work, she wiped her hands on her red pirate coat and set off for Freddie's dorm room.

Needless to say, CJ slept well that night.

HARDY-HAR-HAR

It's been a long time since
I pulled a good prank.

I'd forgotten how wicked awesome it feels.

CJ refused to use an alarm clock. Even when they didn't tick, clocks weren't her thing. But the next morning, she had no trouble getting up. She awoke with the sun and found a good hiding spot in a tall tree near the locker banks where she could watch the morning drama unfold.

It wasn't long before students began filing out of the banquet hall and grabbing books from their lockers. CJ smiled as she watched Audrey strut to her locker and attempt to open the door.

Obviously, it didn't open.

Audrey tugged harder, even letting out a dainty grunt, but the glue held strong. CJ covered her mouth to keep herself from laughing aloud and giving away her position.

Then King Ben noticed Audrey's struggling and went to help. He tried to pull the locker door open, but he couldn't get it to budge, either. Jay, Jafar's son, who CJ knew from the Isle of the Lost, joined the effort.

As the three of them pulled, the glue finally gave way and the locker door flew open. That was when the dead fish CJ had planted on the top shelf flew out, smacking Audrey right in the head.

Audrey screamed and started jumping up and down, shrieking, "Get it off! Eeew! Get it off!" It seemed to be caught in her hair.

CJ giggled softly. This was going even better than she'd expected.

As the commotion continued and Ben tried to calm Audrey down, CJ quietly climbed out of her tree and strolled away.

Okay, that was fun, she thought. *Time to get back to work, though.*

As much fun as the fish prank had been, CJ was

worried. Despite her best efforts, she knew she was running out of options. She'd searched everywhere—every garden and classroom. She'd turned over every stone she could find, but she uncovered nothing that even remotely related to treasure.

After almost a week of exploring and eavesdropping, she was starting to realize how her father had felt when he was relentlessly trying to track down Peter Pan in Never Land. He had nearly lost his entire crew because of that fixation. Her father had always been obsessive. As CJ paced the length of Freddie's dorm room early one morning, working herself into a frenzy, she wondered if maybe she had inherited the obsessive gene.

"What are you doing?" Freddie asked from her bed, sounding annoyed. She pulled her pillow over her head to block out the sounds of CJ's restless footsteps.

"I'm thinking."

"You're plotting," Freddie said accusingly.

"Same thing."

Freddie sat up with a sigh. "Will you just tell me what you're up to already?"

Without looking up, CJ waved her friend's question away with her hand. "Go back to sleep."

CJ continued to pace the length of the dorm room.

"The library," she mumbled to herself. "I could go back to the library. But I already searched it twice and there was nothing there. Blast! Why does it have to be so difficult?"

She almost sounded like a crazy person.

Actually, she *did* sound like a crazy person.

"If you tell me what you're up to," Freddie said, pushing off the covers and stretching her arms above her head, "maybe I can help."

CJ stopped pacing and looked at her friend, whose dark pigtailed hair was a mess from her sleeping on it. Maybe she was right. Maybe CJ *could* ask Freddie for help. After all, Freddie went to class every day with the Auradon kids and their teachers. She had access to people who knew things. She could ask questions.

But CJ hated asking for favors. She hated asking for help, period. Her father had taught her that sidekicks were a waste of time. They only got in the way and ruined everything you tried to accomplish. Her father had almost been eaten by a crocodile because of his sidekick's ineptness. And he'd been terrified of crocodiles ever since. It was a fear that ran in the family.

But CJ was at the end of her rope. It was becoming clearer every day that she couldn't do this by herself.

"Well," CJ said, her mouth stretching open in a big yawn, "I guess if you really wanted to help—you know, if it meant *that* much to you—*maybe* you could ask around to see if anyone knows where a tulip so bold or a special stone unturned can be found."

Freddie crossed her arms over her chest. "Why?"

CJ shrugged and adjusted her golden-brown ponytail in the mirror. "No reason. Just curious. I've become somewhat of a botany scholar."

"No, you haven't," Freddie said.

CJ huffed. "Just ask, okay?" she snapped.

Anyone else might have taken offense at CJ's tone, but not Freddie. She just smirked. "No."

CJ felt her temper flare. She reminded herself to stay calm, play it cool. "Freddsie," she pleaded in a syrupy tone, plastering on a fake smile. "C'mon. Help a matey out, would ya? Just ask someone. It'll take two secs."

Freddie stood up and started getting dressed for class. "I don't *need* to ask anyone. I already know where the tulip so bold and the special stone unturned are."

CJ's arms fell limp at her sides. "You do?"

Freddie slipped her feet into her boots and adjusted the tiny purple top hat on her head. "Yup. We learned about them in Auradon Geography class the other day."

She started walking toward the door. "Well, I'm off to—"

But CJ dashed in front of her, blocking her exit. "Wait. Freddie, old chum. Let's talk."

Freddie smirked again. "Yes. Let's." Then the smile fell from her face. "Tell me what you're plotting and I'll tell you what I know."

CJ stomped her boot on the floor. "Why won't you just tell me?"

"Why won't *you*?" Freddie shot back.

CJ could feel her face getting warm. It did that, turning bright red, when she got mad. And she was *mad*. What kind of friend was Freddie, withholding valuable information from her? That was just cruel, and not in the fun way.

"I . . ." CJ struggled to speak. "I'm . . ." But she couldn't get the words out. Sure, Freddie was her best friend, but this was her biggest secret ever. She couldn't just come out and *tell* someone.

"Well," Freddie practically sang, "I'm off to music class. I'm working on a new song, and I want to scarf down some of those delicious cream puffs for breakfast first." She flashed CJ a sickeningly cheesy smile and waved. "Lates!"

"Ugh! You're so evil!" exclaimed CJ.

"Thank you!" Freddie called as she closed the door.

CJ grunted. What had gotten into her friend? She was acting like an AK—short for "Auradon Kid"—and it had barely been a week! Music class? Cream puffs? That girl really needed to sort out her priorities.

As she listened to her friend's vanishing footfalls on the other side of the door, CJ knew she needed to come up with a new plan. If Freddie wouldn't tell her what the stone unturned was, she'd have to seek out the answer another way.

And she knew instantly that it would involve one of her favorite pastimes—breaking and entering.

SINK ME!

Blarg! Freddie's such a swab!

Whatever. I don't need her.
I can do this on my own.

That night, after everyone had gone to sleep, CJ slipped outside.

She tied the end of a rope she'd stolen from the gym into a loop and tossed it toward the roof of the castle. It took three tries, but she was finally able to hook it around something. She gave it a quick tug, making sure it was secure, and then began to climb up the side of the building. Climbing ropes was one of CJ's strengths—it was an important skill for a pirate to have—but whatever the rope was attached to on the roof must have not been very sturdy, because just as she reached the third floor, she felt it give way.

Suddenly, CJ was falling. She let out a yelp and grappled for something to hold on to, scraping her knees. Fortunately, her fingertips caught a windowsill just before she plummeted to the ground, and she was able to pull herself up onto a ledge.

That was close, CJ thought.

Falling was definitely *not* part of her plan.

CJ knew that Mal and Evie would sleep with their dorm room door locked. (It was a VK—short for "Villain Kid"—thing. Growing up on the Isle of the Lost, you couldn't trust anyone, even your own parents.) But their window, she was happy to discover, was wide open.

With the deftness of a cat, she slunk inside. Mal and Evie were sound asleep. Evie had a sewing machine set up at her desk, where she'd clearly been working on a new dress for the Neon Lights Ball.

CJ rolled her eyes. Evie was the worst of them all. She had that Evil Queen vainness in her blood. CJ and Evie had never been very close back on the island. CJ couldn't stand to listen to the girl blab about meeting a prince and marrying a prince and moving into a giant castle with a prince. *(Groan.)*

Mal was different, though. She was rotten to the core. At least, she *used* to be. She was the daughter of the most evil villain on the entire island. But this place had gotten to her, too. And if Auradon Prep could get to the daughter of Maleficent, CJ had very little hope for her friend Freddie.

CJ crept silently toward Evie's dresser and started opening drawers. That was another thing about Auradon: Nothing squeaked. Nothing creaked. Nothing had even a spot of dirt on it. It wasn't like the island, where *everything* was old and rusty and complained when you disturbed it. The hinges at Auradon shone with newness. The doors and cupboards were polished and quiet. She even caught sight of her reflection in the floors of the bathroom.

CJ located Evie's magic mirror in the second drawer. It was small—barely bigger than her palm—and framed in gold. She'd seen Evie carrying it around with her everywhere she went. The girl clung to that thing like the AKs clung to their phones.

The mirror had never worked on the island, but CJ

knew that it worked at Auradon. She'd witnessed Evie using it on multiple occasions, speaking clearly into the reflective glass to request that the mirror show her what she wanted to see. Maybe, just maybe, it would work for CJ.

She swallowed and racked her brain for the right thing to say. "Uh," she barely whispered. "Um. Okay. Mirror mirror, in my hand, show me the path to the treasure land."

She peered into the glass, waiting with bated breath. But all she saw was her own annoyed reflection staring back at her. She rolled her eyes again, feeling ridiculous.

If only Daddy could see me now, talking to a stupid mirror.

But she needed that gold. She wanted that ship. So she swallowed her pride and tried again, keeping her voice low. "Mirror, mirror, wise and learned, where is the magic stone unturned?"

"What are you doing?" someone said, and CJ jumped, nearly dropping the mirror. She dove to the ground and scrambled under Evie's bed. With her heart in her throat, she waited for the voice to come again. But all she heard was a snort.

A snort?

Who was snorting?

CJ cocked an eyebrow and slowly peeked her head out from under the bed. It was dark in the room, but a sliver of moonlight from the open window was cast directly across Mal's face. Her eyes were closed and her purple hair was fanned out over her pillow. CJ waited, watching.

Then Mal spoke: "*Fab-mazing* is *not* a real word."

CJ sighed. It was just Mal talking in her sleep. CJ climbed out from under the bed and glared at the mirror in frustration. It must work only for Evie. Talk about the *un*fairest of them all.

She slipped the mirror back into the drawer. Then she peered around the room, searching for something else that might prove useful. She was just about to give up and head back to the open window when she caught sight of something on Mal's bedside table. A book. At first she thought it was Mal's spell book—which she realized wouldn't work for her, either—but as she crept closer and studied the cover, she could see it was something else.

Mal's diary!

She grabbed it and eagerly flipped through the pages, reading about when Mal met Ben, King Beast's son, and the first time she looked into those big doe eyes. *(Ick, please.)* Next CJ skimmed the parts about Mal and Evie's getting settled into their dorm room and their visit to the Museum of Cultural History with Jay and Carlos to try to steal Fairy Godmother's wand.

That was when CJ stopped and her heart started to race.

In this historic site of the learned
Lies a special stone unturned.

The Museum of Cultural History.
History.
A knowing smile crossed CJ's face.

FIRE IN THE HOLE

The museum! Duh!

Now how do I sneak in?
Time to plot again . . .

From reading Mal's diary, CJ learned about the heavy-duty security at the museum.

It was much better than the security at Auradon Prep. According to Mal's account of their thwarted effort to steal Fairy Godmother's wand, the Museum of Cultural History had guards, alarms, security cameras, and even high-tech force fields.

This was not going to be a simple operation. CJ needed a strategy.

After breakfast the next day, the entire school headed

outside to the field for something called tourney. As far as CJ could tell, it was some kind of competitive sport. Curious about this mysterious activity, CJ crept outside and hid under one of the bleachers to observe the action.

But after a few minutes of watching a ball get batted around by wooden paddles and people being randomly tackled, she realized the sport made no sense to her. Then again, neither did cheerleading. She was about to leave when something caught her eye. On the other side of the field, a person was jumping up and down and cheering. But it wasn't just a normal person.

It was a knight. A medieval knight. With metal armor and a helmet and everything. It looked just like all the knight statues she'd seen around Auradon Prep. After all, the Fighting Knight was the school's mascot.

Just then, a whistle blew and the tourney players ran off the field for a short break. At that moment, the knight removed its helmet, and CJ saw who was *inside* the costume. It was Jane, Fairy Godmother's daughter.

CJ was shocked. Jane was so meek and dainty CJ never would have believed it was *her* jumping up and down inside all that heavy armor.

But it gave CJ an idea.

If CJ hadn't been able to tell that Jane was inside

the costume, then no one would be able to tell if *she* was inside the costume, either.

It was the perfect disguise for sneaking into the Museum of Cultural History. According to Mal's diary, there were knight statues all over that museum. CJ would blend right in.

It's a good thing the people of Auradon are so obsessed with knights in shining armor. Although, I have to admit, the costume looks a little dull.

PIRATE IN
SHINING ARMOR

Plan to infiltrate museum:
first this pirate's got to
become a knight!

Does this armor make me look swashbuckling?
'Cause it's a little restricting.

It was the morning of the Neon Lights Ball.

CJ decided that was the best time to infiltrate the museum—when everyone was distracted by preparations for the dance. CJ wasted no time in using her trusty rope again to sneak into Jane's dorm room and locate the costume. It was, by far, the most interesting item of clothing in that room. Every other garment in

Jane's closet was covered in revolting pink bows.

She grabbed the knight costume, practically sinking under its weight. Then, just to keep the Auradon Prep reality show interesting, CJ left a little piece of evidence on the floor—a bracelet of Mal's that she'd swiped from her room the other night. She didn't feel at all guilty framing Mal for stealing the costume. It served the girl right for deserting her Isle friends to run off with the doe-eyed, mad-for-plaid King Ben, son of their greatest enemy. Had Mal completely forgotten who had banished them all to the island to begin with?

Getting her hands on the costume was simple. The problem, CJ soon discovered, was taking it with her. She couldn't hold on to the thing while she slid down the rope. It was far too heavy. So she had no choice but to put it on.

CJ had climbed ropes her entire life. But climbing a rope in a thirty-pound steel knight costume was something else entirely. She could barely grip the rope in her gauntlets, and she couldn't really see where she was going through the small slit cut into the helmet. She nearly plummeted five times.

She was thankful everyone was in the banquet hall for breakfast, because she was sure a medieval knight descending the castle wall on a rope would be quite a sight.

When she finally collapsed inside her room, she was sweaty and out of breath. "Blimey!" she swore, tearing off the helmet and tossing it aside with a noisy clank. "This treasure better be worth it."

"Treasure?" someone with a velvety voice said, startling her. CJ spun around to see Freddie sitting on her bed with a book.

CJ clenched her gloved fists and cursed herself for saying that aloud. Of course anything relating to money or riches would get Freddie's attention. She was Dr. Facilier's daughter, after all.

Freddie closed the book and stood up. *"Interesting,"* she said, elongating the word so that it seemed to go on forever.

CJ rolled her eyes, attempting to ignore her friend.

"Although," Freddie went on, leaning back to admire CJ's costume, "not as interesting as that outfit."

"Oh, shut up," CJ snapped.

"Whatever it is you're doing," Freddie said, "I want in."

"No way."

"I'll tell," Freddie threatened.

But CJ stood her ground. It was easy to do wearing thirty pounds of metal. Besides, she recognized an empty threat when she heard one. "No, you won't."

Freddie scowled. "How do you know I won't?"

"Because if you tell everyone I'm here, you'll have to tell them how I got here and where I've been hiding this whole time. And then you'll get kicked out, too."

Freddie looked stumped and CJ felt a small inkling of pride. She loved winning almost more than she loved gold.

"Freddsie," CJ coaxed in a silky tone, although it didn't have quite the effect she was hoping for, since she was still wearing the ridiculous knight costume. "I'm a *pirate*. And you're"—she gestured ambiguously toward Freddie—"well, whatever it is you are."

"Shadow sorceress," Freddie said, folding her arms.

"Sure, whatevs."

CJ attempted to pull off the top half of the costume, but she could barely get the chest plate over her head. She gave up with a sigh, letting the armor clank back down around her torso. "Anyway," she went on, trying to sound undeterred, "like I was saying, I'm a pirate. Finding treasure is what we do."

Freddie opened her mouth to argue, but CJ cut her off. "And no, I don't need any help, thank you very much. Sidekicks are not really my thing." She hobbled to the bed, making a *clank, clank, clank* with every step. CJ wondered how Jane was able to jump up and down in that thing when she could barely walk in it.

Exhausted, CJ attempted to sit down. But that was a lost cause. The knees of the suit didn't bend very well, and she ended up toppling back onto the bed with an *"oomph."*

Freddie let out an evil laugh. Frustrated, CJ tried to push herself back up, grabbing on to the bedpost for support, but her metal-gloved hand couldn't get a grip, and all she managed to do in the end was make herself sweatier and more breathless. She sank back onto the bed with a surrendering sigh.

"Well," Freddie said breezily, "I'm off to meet the girls for tea. Carlos and Jay are picking us up on a flying carpet. How bad is that?"

CJ let out a harrumph.

"Anyhoo . . ." Freddie went on. Her singsongy tone was really starting to bug CJ. "I guess I'll see ya latsies!"

"Wait," CJ called from the bed, trying and failing

once again to pull herself to a sitting position. "Help me up, will ya?"

Freddie clucked twice. "I thought you said you didn't need any help," she crooned. And with that, she disappeared into the hall.

IT'S TIME TO HAUL WIND!

It's just walking.

How hard can it be?

After a struggle, CJ finally managed to get herself out the window of the dorm room.

Normally the walk to the museum would take twenty minutes. But that was when you *weren't* wearing thirty pounds of armor and getting stopped every few seconds by people who thought you were Jane.

"Hi, Jane!"

"Where are you going, Jane?"

"Hey, Jane! Is there a tourney game tonight?"

If I never have to wear this costume again, it'll be too

soon, CJ thought as she waddled awkwardly down the road.

But the worst part was when Carlos's stupid dog, Dude, spotted her and started barking furiously. As though he *knew* she was an imposter. She kept walking, thinking if she just ignored the dog, it would go away.

But apparently, dogs didn't work like that.

The dog started to chase her.

"Walk the plank, dog! Get lost!"

CJ attempted to pick up the pace, running as best she could in a suit with knees that didn't really bend. She imagined that was what a pirate with a peg leg felt like. The dog yapped and bit at her heels, prompting CJ to *attempt* to run faster. Her legs were aching, and every step made her feel like she was going to fall over.

The one good thing about being pursued by the dog was that she arrived at the museum a lot faster than she'd expected. CJ just managed to squeeze through the front doors and close them behind her before Dude could follow her inside.

The loud noise of the door slamming startled the portly guard in a blue uniform who was sitting at a desk surrounded by security monitors. He looked up and CJ froze on the spot, keeping her body rigid under the costume. Through the tiny slit in her helmet, she could see the guard looking her way, his eyes raking her over. He was probably trying to figure out if that knight had been there just a second earlier. But, no doubt because there were so many knights decorating the halls of the place, he seemed to decide quickly that it was nothing to be alarmed about and turned back to his screens.

CJ blew out a breath and carefully began to creep through the lobby, slowly making her way toward the museum directory that hung on the wall. But the costume was incredibly noisy, clanking with every step CJ took, and the guard repeatedly looked up to see where the sound was coming from. Every time, CJ froze in place, her costume blending in seamlessly with the museum's decor.

When she reached the directory, she had to tilt her head so she could read it through the small opening in her helmet. She scanned the list of exhibits—*Crown of Auradon, Gallery of Heroes, Gallery of Villains*—trying to figure out which one would most likely feature a stone unturned or a tulip so bold.

She was starting to get frustrated with the offerings, until she got three-quarters of the way down the list and a zing of adrenaline shot through her.

That had to be it. Where else would a tulip so bold be found?

Fortunately, the exhibit was on the first floor. The thought of going up and down stairs in the knight getup was too much for CJ to bear.

The *Plants of Enchanted Forests* exhibit was set up in a spacious greenhouse attached to the main building of the museum. As CJ tramped through it in her noisy costume, she caught sight of small illuminated placards posted next to the various plants, flowers, and shrubs, identifying each of the species and where they came from.

She passed by a mangled knot of Maleficent's evil thorns, a pumpkin patch said to have originated from *the* pumpkin used by Fairy Godmother to get Cinderella to the ball, and a small pond covered in floating lily pads that were famous for being hopped on by Princess Tiana and Prince Naveen. CJ smiled at the reminder of Freddie's dad's voodoo spell. He always bragged that turning those two into frogs was some of his best work.

When CJ finally reached the small flower garden positioned in the center of the exhibit, she stopped, looking beneath her feet to see a path made of smooth paving stones.

Stones.

She read the small placard nearby and learned that she had entered the Golden Afternoon Flowerbed. A moment later, she located a bed of brightly colored tulips, labeled with another glowing plaque.

LITTLE BREAD-AND-BUTTERFLIES

KISS THE TULIPS.

Kiss the tulips?

CJ pulled the treasure map out from under her armor and read the second half of the clue again.

Find it among the tulips so bold
And your future will shine bright with gold.

Tulips so bold?

As in bold enough to kiss butterflies?

CJ's heart raced. She was so close she could feel it in her bones. Pirates had to have very good instincts. They had to be able to sense when they were close to a buried treasure, and CJ's senses were on high alert.

She reached for the paver stone closest to the tulip bed and, with one giant heave, lifted the stone and flipped it over.

There, pressed into the dirt beneath the now-turned stone, was a golden key.

YO HO HO!

It's mine! All mine!

I now hold the key to the treasure!
(Evil laugh)

CJ grabbed the key and held it up, flashing a wild grin. And then the obvious question crossed her mind.

What am I supposed to do *with the key?*

She glanced around the greenhouse but she couldn't find anything that seemed to require a key. No treasure chests. No mysterious-looking locks. She peered down at the object in her metal-gloved hand. Her discovery no longer seemed like a victory. Now it was just confusing.

"What do I do with you?" she asked quietly.

She couldn't really crawl in the mascot costume, so

she rolled onto her belly and, careful not to run over the map, slithered around the flowerbed, her hands groping for a clue, something that would help her figure out where she was supposed to insert the key.

But after slithering in a complete circle, she was still at a loss.

That was when she noticed the paver stone she had flipped over lying on the ground next to her. She'd been so distracted by the key itself she hadn't even noticed that there were words written on the underside of the stone.

Curious, CJ tilted her head to read them.

NOTHING IS CARVED IN STONE.

She almost had to laugh at the absurdity of the sentence. Nothing was carved in stone? But those very words were carved right into the stone.

"Nothing is carved in stone," she said, hoping it would make more sense to her if spoken aloud. But she still couldn't figure out the meaning.

Then, out of the corner of her helmet opening, she saw a flicker of movement. She whipped her head to the left, causing the armor to screech. And that was when she saw it.

The map.

It was changing.

There was something about those words on the stone. Saying them aloud had triggered the magic. They had unlocked something, just as CJ's coming to Auradon had.

Eagerly she sat up, grabbed the map, and stared at it.

It was as though invisible hands were drawing right on the page, expanding the kingdom of Auradon before her very eyes. The ghostly artist crafted forests and rivers and mountains. It erected more buildings and more towns, traveling upward from the city of Auradon, connecting long, winding rivers with landmarks that hadn't been there before.

Then a single object—a lake—appeared among the scenery. The invisible artist seemed to take extra care in drawing it, as though it was more special than the rest of the locations that had been sketched.

Once the lake was complete, CJ watched the dotted trail start to expand. More tiny dots appeared as it carved a path through the trees and valleys, around

Belle and Beast's castle, beyond Auradon Prep, and to the lake.

And then . . . nothing.

The invisible hands just *stopped*, as though the artist had run out of ink.

All that time she had thought just stepping foot in Auradon would reveal the entire kingdom. The entire map. But even after turning this special stone, the page was still not entirely filled in. The map was still woefully unfinished.

Blasted barnacles! she thought with a sudden realization. Obviously the map had been enchanted to reveal itself a section at a time. Arriving in Auradon had been the first step. Turning the stone had been the second. And now apparently she needed to go to this mysterious lake to unlock the next part of the map.

But what was she supposed to do once she got there?

She held the map up close to her helmet and scanned the newly revealed trail for another clue, something that would give her more information. But unlike the clue that had led her to the stone, there was nothing to guide her. Just that long, curving series of dots leading to the unidentified body of water.

She sighed and twisted her mouth in concentration.

How was she going to find the lake if she didn't even know what it was called? Sure, she had the dotted trail on her map, but without a compass, it would be almost impossible to find.

What she really needed was some kind of Auradon expert. Or at the very least, someone who knew more about the lay of the land than she did.

But who could she trust to ask?

With a scowl, CJ suddenly remembered Freddie saying something about taking an Auradon geography class.

She slumped in her armor.

She *really* wanted to do this on her own and claim all the glory (and gold) for herself. But Freddie was enrolled as a student at Auradon Prep. She knew more about the kingdom than CJ did. She could be a valuable asset. Plus, Freddie was her best friend, even if she had started singing all the time and hanging out with the AKs.

With a sigh, CJ dropped the map onto the ground next to her, kicking up a cloud of pollen. She closed her mouth tightly and held her breath, but it was too late: she had already inhaled. The pollen was tickling her nose. She could feel a sneeze welling up inside her like a hurricane ready to blow through a harbor.

Just then, the doors of the greenhouse swung open and the capped head of the stocky guard appeared over the top of Maleficent's thornbush. "Hello?" he called out. "Anyone in here?"

CJ froze, trying to remain as still as possible, trying to lock the sneeze inside. But it was rising in her chest, making her eyes water and her fingers tingle. She couldn't hold it back any longer. It exploded out of her in a thundering *ACHOOOOOO!*

The guard spun in her direction. She could see only the top of his head, but she knew he was heading her way. She hastily rolled up the map and stuffed it, along with the gold key, under the breastplate of her armor.

She scrambled to her feet. If she could just get to the other side of the greenhouse, she could hide behind one of the trees and sneak out while the guard was still searching. But her armor thwarted her once again and she fell onto her back.

The stocky guard stepped into the Golden Afternoon Flowerbed and CJ went rigid again.

"Huh," the guard said, approaching her. "This one must have fallen over."

He bent down and started to lift CJ to her feet,

grunting from the effort. "Merlin's beard, this is a heavy one."

CJ gritted her teeth behind her helmet, resisting the urge to hit him.

She held her breath as the guard hoisted her onto her feet and carried her awkwardly toward the nearest wall of the greenhouse, then set her upright.

"There we go," he said to himself, brushing dirt from his hands and turning to leave.

CJ let out the breath she had been holding. But as soon as she did, she felt another monstrous sneeze coming on. She peered through her helmet at the guard. He was taking his sweet time strolling back through the garden.

Hurry! She urged him silently. *Hurry up and—*
ACHOOOOOO!

She nearly toppled over from the force of the thing. The guard spun back around, looking this way and that. CJ knew she was totally fish food now.

Then she heard something in the distance. It sounded like . . .

A dog barking?

Dude! He was still there!

Keeping as still as possible, she felt around the wall at her back for a door she'd noticed earlier. A moment later, her gloved hand brushed against a latch.

With her heart hammering, she yanked hard on the handle, and a hidden door flew open. Dude zoomed into the greenhouse, yapping his scruffy head off. He was so focused on his entrance he didn't even see CJ standing there in her knight costume. But he *did* lay eyes on the guard.

Woof! Woof! Woof!

With renewed purpose, Dude took off in the direction of the guard. The man yelped and started running. CJ grinned and slipped out of the greenhouse, shutting the door quietly behind her.

And that, mateys, is what pirates call docking two ships with one anchor.

UNFURLING THE MAP

I don't do sidekicks.

But I guess if I'm going to ask anyone for help, Freddie is the best choice.

"So let me get this straight," Freddie said, staring at the map CJ had unrolled on her bed in their dorm room. "You stole this map from your father's study; two portions of it have already been unlocked; you found a mysterious key at the museum; and you're on this wild pirate treasure hunt?"

CJ touched the gold key, which she had hung around her neck on a string the moment she had gotten back from the museum and changed out of that stupid knight costume.

"Yes," she replied, confirming all the things she had revealed to Freddie. Her gut was churning. She'd never told anyone about the map before, let alone *shown* it to someone. And here she was with her biggest secret unfurled on her bed while Freddie stood there gawking at it.

What if Freddie really had become an AK? What if she turned her in? What if King Beast confiscated the map, the way he'd confiscated her dad's precious gold compass, and dragged her back to the Isle of the Lost? Then she really *would* be lost. She'd be stuck there without a way off the island and without her precious treasure map. And she couldn't afford to lose her map. It was the only way she was going to get her ship!

No, she thought, trying to assure herself. *Freddie would never do that to me.*

Would she?

"So," Freddie went on, "you haven't been stowing away in my dorm room just to terrorize the school?"

CJ grinned. "No, that's just been a perk."

"This whole time you've really been searching for some kind of buried treasure?"

CJ nodded once, looking smug.

"And you've suddenly decided to tell me this *why*?"

CJ slumped onto the bed next to the map. "As it

turns out," she began, avoiding Freddie's piercing gaze, "I sort of, kind of, maybe just a little bit need your help." She mumbled the last three words, making them nearly impossible to understand.

CJ knew Freddie was smiling. She could practically hear it. "I'm sorry," Freddie said, taking a step closer. "I didn't quite catch that last part. What did you say?"

CJ rolled her eyes and scuffed her foot against the floor. "I. Need. Your. Help," she finally spit out. "There. Happy?"

She braved a look at Freddie, who was beaming.

"Why, yes," Freddie said, exaggerating her southern accent, "I believe I *am* quite happy right now."

"Don't be so smug." CJ crossed her arms. "I'm only asking because you know more about the United States of Auradon than I do." She gestured helplessly toward the map. "I don't even know what that lake is!"

Freddie leaned forward to examine the map. Her eyes traveled along the path of the dotted trail until it ended at the mysterious body of water.

"It's the Enchanted Lake," Freddie said knowingly. "Mal and Ben went there on their first date."

CJ huffed. If she had just read a little farther in Mal's diary, maybe she would have figured that out herself.

"So you'll take me there, right?" CJ asked.

Freddie frowned. "You want me to leave Auradon Prep and risk getting caught *and* exiled back to the Isle of the Lost just to help you dig up some old box?"

CJ felt her temper flaring and her face growing hot. She grabbed a fistful of the blanket on the bed to keep from exploding. "It's not just an old box," she growled through gritted teeth. "It's a treasure. And I'm going to use it to buy my own ship."

Freddie crossed her arms. "And what do I get out of it?"

CJ batted her eyelashes. "The extreme satisfaction of helping out your bestie," she said in her best princess impersonation. "Isn't that reward enough for an AK?"

Freddie narrowed her eyes at the insult. "I might go to school here, but I am *not* an AK."

"Could've fooled me," CJ said out of the side of her mouth as she cast her gaze to the floor.

CJ could sense that Freddie was starting to cave, which meant it was time to drop the anchor. "I mean," CJ went on, trying her best to sound innocent and not like she was purposefully manipulating her best friend, which, of course, she was, "if you'd rather stay around here all day learning about the history of ruffles instead of helping out your partner in crime, then go ahead. I get it. I really do. You've changed. A week at Auradon Prep has transformed you, forced you to see the error in your wicked ways. That's fine. I'll just—"

"When would we leave?" Freddie asked.

CJ did her best to hide her triumphant smile.

Hook, line, and sinker.

"Now's as good a time as ever!" CJ said.

Freddie shook her head. "Nuh-uh. The Neon Lights Ball is tonight. I helped come up with the theme. And my dress is killer. I'm not going to miss it."

CJ fought hard not to roll her eyes. She was so tired of everyone talking about that stupid Neon Lights Ball. "Fine, tomorrow morning, then."

"And we're *partners* in crime," Freddie confirmed. "Like you said. None of this captain/first mate nonsense."

CJ waved that away like it was the most ridiculous thing she'd ever heard. "Of course we're *partners*."

Freddie scrutinized CJ for a long time, as though she were trying to place some Dr. Facilier–style truth spell on her. CJ kept the innocent smile frozen on her face until her cheeks started to burn.

"Okay," Freddie said with a sigh. "But I'm not going to take orders from you. I'm not your Smee."

CJ snorted. "I wouldn't *dream* of giving you orders." Excited, she leapt to her feet, rolled up the map, and stuffed it into her coat pocket. "Now start getting ready," she commanded. "We leave at dawn."

ALL HANDS ON DECK!

Today we cast off for the Enchanted Lake!

If only it came with an enchanted ship.

The next morning, before anyone was awake, CJ crept out of the building. She needed to secure transportation for her and Freddie. And she knew exactly where to find it.

A few minutes later, Freddie walked down the front steps of the castle to find CJ sitting atop a black-and-white motor scooter.

Freddie's mouth fell open. "Is that Ben's Vespa?"

"Yup!" CJ replied proudly. "And how wicked do I look on it?" She struck various angry-pirate poses.

Freddie looked skeptical. "Do you even know how to drive that thing?"

CJ waved her concern away. "Child's play. If I can steer a ship, I can drive a scooter."

"But you've never actually *steered* a ship," Freddie pointed out.

CJ scoffed. "Steering ships is in my blood. Besides, you've never turned anyone into a frog, but that doesn't mean you can't."

Freddie thought about that. "Actually, I think that's exactly what it means."

CJ ignored her friend's protests. "Hop on!"

Freddie walked around the Vespa, inspecting it like a mechanic. Then she shrugged, swung her leg over the seat, and wrapped her arms around CJ's red coat.

CJ revved the engine, letting out a loud whoop, and they took off.

CJ loved the feeling of the wind in her face as she drove. It wasn't exactly a pirate ship, but it was close enough.

"Isn't this fun?" she called back to Freddie.

But Freddie didn't reply, and CJ thought she might still be mad about the previous night. CJ had decided to crash the Neon Lights Ball. And Freddie wasn't too happy about it, because now the AKs knew Freddie had been hiding CJ in her dorm room the whole time. But CJ had grown bored waiting around. What else was she supposed to do stuck in that castle with a treasure map burning a hole in her pocket while Freddie and her new friends danced the night away?

Whatever, CJ thought. *Freddie will get over it eventually.*

As they drove through the Auradon countryside, Freddie yelled directions in CJ's ear, but CJ was set on going her own way.

"Why did you even bring me if you weren't going to listen to me?" Freddie yelled over the wind.

"I'm a pirate," CJ yelled back. "We have excellent navigation skills."

"But you don't even have a compass," Freddie pointed out. "How do you know we're going the right way?"

CJ scowled. *That was a low blow.* Leave it to Freddie to bring up a sore spot like the compass. Freddie *knew* CJ's father's compass had been taken when he was sent to the island. And she *knew* how painful that had been for him.

"Well," CJ shot back bitterly, "you don't have any shadow cards, so you can't read the future."

"I don't need shadow cards to know that we're going the wrong way."

"You said the lake is due east from the castle. We're going east."

CJ was thankful Freddie remained silent after that. She didn't even gloat when CJ got them totally lost and they ended up at the Museum of Antiquities, which was *north* of the castle, not east.

Well, she didn't gloat *much*, anyway. CJ tried her best to ignore the "I told you so" look on Freddie's face after a gardener told them they weren't even close and pointed them in the right direction.

As they sped down the road under a gorgeous canopy of pine trees, Freddie started to sing on the back of the bike. CJ immediately recognized the song as one Freddie used to sing back on the Isle of the Lost. But CJ had never realized how catchy the song was, and before she knew it, she was singing along.

A half hour later, after they'd sung nearly every song CJ knew the words to, CJ started to notice something odd about their surroundings.

This can't be right, she thought with a frown as she pulled the bike to a stop. The road had grown narrow, and there was a thicket of trees all around them.

Freddie started to kick off another song, but CJ quickly shushed her. "I think we're lost again."

"No," Freddie said nonchalantly. "We're here." She removed her helmet, hopped off the Vespa, and started marching into the trees. "The lake is this way."

"How do you know?" CJ called to Freddie.

"My magic shadow cards told me!" Freddie called back sarcastically. Then, a second later, she added, "We learned about it in geography. Come on!"

CJ switched off the bike's engine, removed her helmet, and hung it on the handlebar of the Vespa. "What about the bike?" she called after Freddie. "We can't just leave it here. Someone will pinch it."

Freddie laughed. "We're in *Auradon*, remember? People here only use the word *pinch* when they're talking about cookie recipes."

CJ glanced one more time at the bike, hoping Freddie was right, before trudging into the woods after her friend.

They seemed to walk forever, and just when CJ was about to smugly point out that this time *Freddie* had been the one to get them lost, they came upon a long rickety bridge suspended over a great ravine.

As they crossed, CJ glanced over the side at the river

running beneath them. In the distance, she could see a gushing wall of tumbling water. She stopped for a moment, mesmerized by the sight. She'd never seen a waterfall in real life, only in her imagination.

Her father used to tell her stories about living in Never Land, back when he was the most evil and feared pirate in the world. He told her about all the vibrant trees and rocky cliffs, the islands shaped like giant skulls and the dangerous coves named after cannibals, the sparkling colors and walls of falling water. But until now, CJ had never believed that a wall could actually be made out of water. It seemed impossible.

"Doesn't look like the Isle of the Lost, does it?" Freddie said, stepping up next to her to admire the view.

CJ shook her head, unable to tear her eyes away from the magnificent sight.

"Kind of makes you want to stay for a while, huh?" Freddie asked.

That immediately broke CJ out of her trance. "Ha, yeah, right," she muttered, and continued across the bridge.

"What's so horrible about this place?" Freddie asked behind her. "I mean, besides the lame AKs?"

"What's so *great* about it?" CJ barked in return.

"Well, it's clean, for starters," Freddie replied. "And the food is much better. My father used to tell me stories about the food in the bayou. Especially the beignets. Fried pockets of dough dusted with powdered sugar. They sounded so amazing."

CJ harrumphed. "A true pirate can survive on nothing but seaweed for months. Besides, I don't have time to think about food. I have a treasure to unbury."

Freddie laughed. "How do you know this treasure really exists?"

"It exists," CJ affirmed.

"How do you *know*?"

"I feel it."

"You *feel* it?" echoed Freddie dubiously.

"It's a pirate thing. You wouldn't understand."

Freddie fell silent for a few seconds, and CJ thought she had finally won the argument, but then Freddie asked, "How do you know it's even still there? What if your dad dug it up years ago, before he was banished to the island?"

They had almost reached the other side of the bridge, but Freddie's comment made CJ pause. She hadn't thought about that before. What if Freddie was right? What if it *had* already been dug up years before? The map, after all, was pretty old. It had been hidden in her father's study for as long as she could remember. What if whoever had hidden the treasure and enchanted the map had changed their mind at some point and gone back to get it?

What if the whole thing was nothing but a fool's errand?

CJ hastily shook the thought away and kept walking. She couldn't afford to think like that. She needed her ship, and that treasure was the only way she was going to get it.

"I just know," she muttered as she stepped off the bridge and continued onto a dirt path leading into another thick forest of trees. But even as she said it, she wondered who she was trying harder to convince, Freddie or herself.

It didn't matter, though. Because a few seconds later, all her worries, anxieties, and doubts suddenly evaporated into thin air as she stepped into a clearing and stared at the majestic site in front of them.

There, nestled among the trees and rocks and wildflowers, sparkling the way she'd always imagined the waters of Never Land sparkled, was the Enchanted Lake.

CANNONBALL!

Okay, so this lake isn't an ocean. But it'll do!

I wonder if there are any crocodiles in it.

CJ ran all the way to the shore of the lake.

Then she had to slow down to keep from falling in. She knelt by the side of the luminous water, which glittered in the sunshine, removed the map from her pocket, and carefully unfolded it. Freddie knelt beside her and they both stared intently at the page.

"Is it supposed to do something?" Freddie whispered, like she was afraid of scaring off the spirits of the map.

"Shhh," CJ ordered her. "Quiet."

"Don't shush me," Freddie griped. "You promised no orders. Partners, remember?"

"Shhh," CJ said again.

They continued to watch the map, riveted. CJ felt her body tingle with anticipation. It had to work. They were at the right spot. This was the Enchanted Lake. So why wasn't the map doing anything?

She gnawed on her lower lip and waited for it to transform again—for those invisible hands to come alive and start drawing, revealing more and more of the world that held her treasure hostage.

But it stayed exactly as it was. CJ was starting to get really frustrated by the map. It was almost as stubborn as she was.

She collapsed onto her butt with a sigh. "It's not working."

"Maybe we're supposed to *do* something," Freddie suggested. "You said when you went to the museum you had to turn over a stone *and* read what was written underneath. Maybe just being here is only half of it."

CJ brightened. "Yes! Exactly. We need to *do* something." A moment later, her mood darkened again. "But what?"

Freddie looked as stumped as CJ felt. They both

glanced around the lake and noticed a small red fox perched on the opposite shore, lapping at the water.

"Maybe we should drink from it," Freddie suggested.

CJ looked into the crystal-clear water and saw a blanket of moss at the bottom. She shrugged. "No worse than the water back on the island, I guess."

"I think this might be cleaner."

They both laughed and leaned forward to scoop some water into their hands. It felt tingly on CJ's skin, like tiny fireflies were floating in it. She looked at Freddie, who looked back at her.

They both shrugged and took a sip. CJ braced herself for the horrible sludgy flavor she endured every time she drank water on the Isle of the Lost. But she was surprised. The water tasted fresh. Clean. Even kind of invigorating. She wondered what drinking from an enchanted lake in Auradon would do to a VK like her. Did it have long-term side effects? Maybe that was what ultimately did Mal in. Maybe the whole time she'd been under an enchanted spell from that lake.

"It's good," Freddie said, mirroring CJ's surprise. "Like really good." Freddie bent over for another sip.

CJ pulled her back. "Let's not risk it."

They both turned toward the map, which was still

lying on the rock beside them. CJ waited again for something to happen.

But again, she was disappointed.

"Hmmm," Freddie said. "Maybe drinking it isn't enough. Maybe we need to, like, you know, get *in* it."

"Ugh. *No*," CJ said, immediately shooting the idea down. "I'm not getting in there."

It was a well-known fact that very few people on the Isle of the Lost could swim. Growing up with a magical barrier keeping everyone landlocked allowed very few opportunities for childhood swim lessons. In fact, most of the kids there were secretly terrified of the water.

Not CJ, obviously. Pirates were born with an affinity for water.

"It doesn't look that deep," Freddie said, prodding. "It's not like you're going to drown."

"Of course I won't *drown*," CJ grunted.

"Then what are you so afraid of?"

CJ kicked at a nearby pebble. It flew off the rock, plunked into the lake, and immediately sank to the bottom. CJ could almost picture herself as that pebble, sinking to the bottom like an anchor.

She abruptly stood up. "Nothing. I'm not afraid of anything."

Freddie stood up, too. "Me neither."

"Great. Then you go first." CJ motioned toward the water.

"No, no, you. I insist," Freddie replied with her velvet voice. "This is *your* treasure hunt. You should really do the honors."

CJ stared into the sparkling abyss, trying to summon the strength to jump. "Together?"

Freddie nodded. "Okay."

"One . . . two . . ."

On *three*, the girls jumped, both letting out screams as their bodies—clothes and all—penetrated the water's surface, sending ripples throughout the entire lake.

CJ flailed helplessly, her arms feeling as useless as a dead squid's tentacles. She cried out, "Help! Help! I'm drowning! I'm . . ." But then she tucked her legs under her, and her feet made contact with the bottom of the lake. She stood up. The water barely came to her waist. "I'm . . . *standing*," she finished in surprise.

Freddie laughed. "You should have seen you. 'Help! Help! I'm drowning!'" She pitched her voice up in a mocking impersonation of CJ.

CJ splashed water toward her. "I do *not* sound like that."

Freddie splashed water back. "You went all damsel in distress there for a second."

CJ let out a scandalized gasp. "You did *not* just call me a damsel in distress."

"Uh," Freddie said, swaying her hips, "actually, I think I did."

CJ, laughing, cupped her hands, dipped them in the water, and flung them toward Freddie. It was a direct hit. Her silky black hair was soaked.

After she'd gotten over the shock of being water-logged, Freddie pressed her lips together and sought her revenge, gathering an even larger handful of water and sending it flying toward CJ. It splashed over her head, drenching her wild ponytail so she looked like a dog after a bath.

"Oh, you'll regret that!" CJ said, moving toward her friend.

Freddie screamed playfully and tried to get away, but it was hard to run in the water, and she ended up falling face-first into the lake. CJ cackled with delight. But Freddie used the opportunity to fill her mouth with water, and when she resurfaced, she sprayed it all over CJ—*and* the rock behind CJ, where the map lay.

The smile from their game washed right off CJ's

face. She spun around, her eyes widening in panic when she saw the droplets of water on her precious map.

"What did you do?" she screeched, wading toward the rock as fast as she could. Her thick red pirate coat billowed behind her in the water, slowing her down.

"I'm sorry," Freddie said, sounding genuinely apologetic as she made her way over.

But CJ held out her hand to stop her. "Don't come any closer," she growled. "You've already done enough."

Careful not to get any more water on the page, CJ leaned forward to assess the damage. Had Freddie completely ruined it? Was the ink bleeding? Could they even still read it?

She let out a small gasp.

"What?" Freddie asked, moving up behind her. "Is it bad? Is it really bad?"

CJ didn't answer. Transfixed, she reached out and took hold of the yellowed paper in her wet, slippery fingers.

Freddie sucked in a sharp breath when she finally saw what CJ had been staring at. "The map," Freddie said, paddling awkwardly through the waist-high water to get a closer look. "Something's happening to it."

THE PIRATE AND
THE FROG

*All this treasure hunting is
what I've always dreamed of.*

And having Freddie as my sidekick isn't so terrible.

CJ and Freddie huddled, dripping wet, around the map, watching it transform.

"Leaping frogs!" Freddie exclaimed.

"Believe me now?" CJ said, bumping Freddie with her shoulder.

But it didn't take long for CJ to recognize that something was wrong. The last time she had watched a new section of the map unlock, it had been revealed in a sort of sweeping motion, like someone was pulling back a curtain. This time, however, only small, random pieces of the map were appearing, like there was a hitch in the magic. It wasn't a smooth, gradual unveiling. It was more like someone was splatter-painting with the ink.

Like someone was sprinkling drops of . . .

"Water!" CJ said with a sudden burst of inspiration. "It was the water!"

In a split-second decision, she held the map firmly between her fingers and submerged the entire thing in the lake.

Freddie's eyes nearly popped right out of her head. "Are you crazy? You're going to destroy it!"

But CJ was two steps ahead of her, because when she withdrew the soaking-wet paper, she could see that her theory was correct. It was the water that was magic. It was the water that unlocked the new area of the map!

"Whoa," Freddie marveled as they both watched the new landscape unfurl before them.

CJ held her breath, hoping that *this* time the picture would be complete, that all the pieces would reveal themselves and the dotted trail would finally end at the location of the treasure.

The map expanded far and wide, revealing a tall mountain to the north and more forest to the east. Then the invisible artist started to travel south, painting small towns and villages along the way, reaching the southern peninsula of the kingdom and a large cove that Freddie instantly recognized.

"The Bayou d'Orleans!" she exclaimed, pointing at the C-shaped curve in the coastline. "That's where my dad's from."

"Oh, good," CJ grumbled. "We can go say hi to Mr. and Mrs. Frog."

She bit her lip and focused hard on the map. The ink had nearly covered the entire piece of paper. What had once been the vast yellowed nothingness of her childhood was almost completely filled in now. The only part that was still missing was an area in the northeast corner of the map.

"C'mon. C'mon," she urged, tightening her grip on the water-soaked paper.

But then, to her grave disappointment, once again, the magic seemed to just run out. The artist stopped mid-stroke, leaving another gaping hole in the picture.

"What's up there?" CJ asked desperately, turning to her friend. She tapped her finger brusquely on the top right corner of the map, directly above the Bayou d'Orleans. "What's here?"

But Freddie just stared blankly back at her. "I don't know. Dad only talked about the bayou. Not what was beyond it."

"But you've been taking Auradon Geography."

"Yeah," Freddie replied scornfully, "for a *week*. Auradon is a big place and we didn't get that far." She bent her head to study the newly transformed map again. "But I do know what *that* is." She pointed to a small village southeast of Auradon Prep, in a region labeled Auroria.

CJ squinted at the name of the town, which had been scrawled there by the invisible artist. " 'Briar's Hollow,' " she read aloud. Then she turned back to Freddie. "Why would I care about some shrimpy little village called Briar's Hollow?"

Freddie rolled her eyes. "Because of that." She moved her finger half an inch up, and CJ finally understood. The dotted trail. It had extended again, from the place they were standing—the Enchanted Lake—winding across the countryside and stopping in the center of the Auroria region, right next to Briar's Hollow.

"So you learned about this town in geography?" CJ asked, feeling excitement beginning to bubble up inside her again.

"No," Freddie said.

CJ was confused. "Then where?"

Freddie groaned. "From Audrey. She talks about that village all the time. You know, Princess Aurora's daughter. Briar Rose. Briar's Hollow. Get it? Apparently, this town was where the woodcutter's cottage was. The one Briar Rose grew up in when she was hiding from Maleficent."

"Coward," CJ muttered.

"Exactly," Freddie agreed. "Audrey said a little town sprung up in those woods after it was revealed that the princess had been living there for sixteen years. It's mostly inhabited by fairies now."

CJ shuddered at the word and practically gulped. "Fairies?" she echoed, hoping her voice wasn't shaking.

If it was, Freddie didn't seem to notice. "Yeah. The girl wouldn't shut up about it." She transformed her voice into a high-pitched mouse-like squeak to impersonate Audrey. "Fairies helped raise me. I have relatives in Briar's Hollow, where the fairies live."

CJ couldn't help snickering at the impression. "You sound just like her."

Freddie sighed. "I think maybe I've been hanging out with AKs too much."

"So you admit coming with me was a *good* idea?"

Freddie pursed her lips. "Okay, I admit I *am* having a little bit of fun."

CJ cocked an eyebrow. "A little bit?"

Freddie just splashed her with more water.

"Hey!" CJ warned, raising the map above her head. "Be careful. You're going to get it wet!"

They both looked at the drenched map that was dripping water into CJ's hair and burst out laughing.

CLOSE TO THE CHEST

We're making progress.

I think?

The girls walked back through the forest and across the bridge to the road.

"So," CJ said, buckling her helmet, "which way to Briar's Hollow?"

"Well, I was thinking," Freddie began, looking thoughtful. "If we're going to get fairies to help us, we're going to have to—"

"Hold up," CJ interrupted, feeling another shudder run through her. "Who said anything about fairies helping us?"

It was one thing to ask her best friend for help; it was quite another to ask *pixies*.

Freddie sighed. "You know, for a pirate's daughter, you're not very observant." She grabbed the map from CJ's hand and began to unroll it, spreading her own hand across the surface to remove the wrinkles.

"Whoa, whoa!" CJ said, grabbing the map. "Easy there. Only the captain gets to handle the treasure map."

Freddie shot her a look.

CJ sighed and gave the map back to her. "Yeah, yeah, partners," she muttered, shaking her head. "Whatever."

"Look," Freddie began, tapping on the part of the dotted trail that led to Briar's Hollow.

"Be careful!" CJ said, lunging forward to push Freddie's hand away. "It's not one of your shadow cards. This thing is super old. And look—you already got it dirty."

Freddie scoffed. "I did not."

"Yes, you did. Look." CJ pointed to a small smudge of dirt at the end of the dotted trail. She tried to lightly brush it away with her hand, but it wouldn't come off. So she went at it with her fingernail, scraping the tattered paper. "What is with this dirt? Why won't it come off?"

"You're going to rip it," Freddie said, pulling the map away from CJ's merciless fingernail. "Just leave it."

CJ crossed her arms. "Fine."

"As I was saying," Freddie went on, "we need a fairy to help us because of *this*."

Freddie aimed her fingertip at a small section of the dotted trail and held the map up so CJ could see it better.

CJ felt a charge of exhilaration when she saw what Freddie was talking about, followed immediately by embarrassment that *she* hadn't been the one to see it first. She was supposed to be the pirate, not Freddie. Why hadn't she noticed the tiny words scrawled just under the dotted trail?

It was exactly the way the first message had been written, in cursive handwriting positioned alongside the curving path. And as CJ twirled her hair and squinted to read it, she knew instantly what it was: another clue. Just like the one that had led her to the museum.

In the tale of Rose, you might recall,
The fairies helped the bad to fall.
When magic shrinks the big to small,
you'll see the final clue of all.

"What does it mean?" CJ asked. She didn't expect Freddie to have an answer. She'd simply been thinking aloud in an attempt to figure it out herself.

But Freddie replied. "It means we need to find a fairy to shrink the map."

"What?" CJ panicked. She grabbed the map from Freddie, hastily rolled it up, and stuffed it safely into her pocket. "No way. I'm not letting any glittery pixies near this thing."

"It's what the clue says to do," Freddie argued. " 'When magic shrinks the big to small, you'll see the final clue of all.' What else could that mean?"

"I'm *not* letting a fairy cast a spell on my map."

Freddie shrugged and examined her fingernails like she was checking them for chipped polish, even though she wasn't wearing any. "That's fine. Whatever. I mean, it's *your* treasure hunt, right? I guess we'll just go back to Auradon Prep and forget the whole thing."

CJ gritted her teeth. Her father had always told her never to trust fairies. It had been ingrained in her just as deeply as her fear of ticking clocks and crocodiles. How could she possibly risk letting a fairy cast a spell on her map?

But did she really have a choice? The clue might have been written somewhat cryptically, but it was pretty clear what it was directing them to do.

She heaved a sigh and tossed her leg over the bike. "Fine. So we'll go to Briar's Hollow and find a fairy to shrink the map. Come on."

Freddie shook her head. "Nuh-uh. We're not going looking like *this*."

CJ peered down at her damp clothes. "Like what?"

"Like VKs! This isn't Auradon Prep, where we're *sort of* tolerated. The rest of the country hasn't exactly gotten on board with King Ben's proclamation to let VKs into Auradon. They still don't trust us."

"So what do you propose we do?" asked CJ.

Freddie nervously scratched her face. "I don't think we have much of a choice. We're going to need to disguise ourselves."

CJ *definitely* didn't like where this was going. "As what?" she asked sharply.

Freddie blew out a long breath. "As Auradon kids."

OVERBOARD

These clothes are definitely not conducive to climbing up a rigging.

Who wears this stuff?

CJ scowled at her reflection in the mirror. "Is this really how AKs dress?"

She and Freddie had driven all the way back to Auradon Prep after Freddie had insisted on returning Ben's Vespa before he realized it was gone. And they'd been able to steal some jelly doughnuts from the kitchen for a snack. Now they were standing inside a small clothing shop in downtown Auradon. It had been closed when they'd arrived, but the door was unlocked, so they'd just entered and helped themselves.

"Yes," Freddie said. "Trust me. I've been hanging out with those people long enough to know that *this* is exactly the kind of thing they would wear."

CJ was sporting a pink-and-blue-striped poofy dress (CJ despised *anything* poofy), a green belt with gold stars on it, a turquoise vest, and purple high heels with daisies on them. CJ much preferred her crocodile-skin pirate boots with the hook-shaped buckles, but Freddie had insisted that floral was much more Auradonian than hooks were. To make matters much worse, Freddie had also attached little pink bows to the entire ensemble, making CJ look like she'd just survived an explosion in a ribbon factory.

"I feel like maybe we went a bit . . . overboard," said CJ.

"We'll blend right in," Freddie assured her, stepping into view in the mirror and bumping her hip against CJ's. Freddie's outfit wasn't much better. She had dressed herself in a yellow-and-blue plaid dress with a pink kimono over it and white knee-high socks with pink ruffles. She'd also replaced her tiny purple top hat with a headband covered in bluebirds. She looked as ridiculous as CJ.

They'd packed all their old VK clothes in backpacks,

except the key CJ had found under the special stone unturned. That was still tied around her neck. She had no idea what it was for, but she wanted it to be close at hand, just in case.

"C'mon," CJ said, pulling on her backpack and heading for the door. She was anxious to get away from that revolting reflection. "We need to figure out how to get—" But the second she stepped outside, she was nearly trampled by a young couple running down the sidewalk.

"Hurry up, darling," the man called out to his wife, who was a few paces behind him, "or we'll miss the bus!"

"I *am* hurrying, darling," the woman replied with an obnoxiously pretentious accent. "Stop rushing me. We paid good money for this bus tour of the kingdom of Auradon. They're not going to simply leave without us."

CJ's gaze followed them up the street and landed on a large silver tour bus idling in the distance. The words *I Can Show You the World . . . of Auradon* were painted on the side, and over the windshield was a sign that read

NEXT STOP: BRIAR'S HOLLOW

"Uh, Freddie," she called back into the shop. Freddie was still admiring her ensemble in the mirror.

"Wouldn't I look positively sinful singing on a stage dressed like this?" Then she started to croon a soulful jazz number.

CJ rolled her eyes. "Freddie!"

"What?" Freddie asked, frowning. "Can't a girl solo for a minute without being interrupted?"

"We don't have a minute. Quit setting the jib and look!" CJ pointed to the husband and wife, who were just stepping aboard the tour bus. CJ flashed her infamous grin. "I think I found our ride. And it's leaving now."

OVERHAUL

Bus ride for two, please.

And no, we're not going to pay.

The driver of the tour bus regarded CJ and Freddie with great skepticism.

"I don't remember you being on this tour," he said. "Are you sure you're in the right place?"

They were standing on the sidewalk, staring into the open door of the bus. CJ pushed Freddie aside. She could take it from there. "Now listen up," she growled. "We can do this the easy way or the hard way."

The driver frowned in confusion. "What's the hard way?"

CJ rolled her eyes. "I tie you all up and take the whole bus hostage. Duh!"

Freddie gently pulled CJ by the shoulders until Freddie was standing in front of the bus door. "Sorry about her," she said quickly in her velvet voice. "She's"—Freddie wheeled her hands around, trying to come up with a good excuse for CJ's behavior—"practicing for a play."

Comprehension dawned on the bus driver's face and his smile returned. "Ah. I see. So you're students?"

"Yes!" Freddie replied in her lilting cadence. "Exactly. And we're studying Auradon geography this semester, so we thought, what better way to *learn* about this great kingdom than to see it ourselves! So we booked this tour."

The driver seemed so mesmerized by Freddie that CJ thought he was about to let them board just like that. But then, as though he were coming out from under a spell, he shook his head. "Where are your tickets, then?"

CJ watched Freddie's smile slide right off her face. "Um . . . uh . . ." she stammered.

CJ butted in. "Some VKs stole them!"

The driver gasped as though she had just shown him a hook hand. "VKs?" His voice trembled. "You mean those awful children King Ben let into the kingdom?"

CJ faked disgust. "The very ones. Can you believe the nerve of that guy? Letting those scoundrels into our boring—" Freddie kicked her. "Er, *beautiful* kingdom?"

The driver shook his head. "I'll never understand that proclamation. Giving the offspring of our enemies access to our homes, our lands, our *children*? Even though Mal turned her mother into a lizard, that doesn't mean evil isn't still in her blood."

CJ snorted. "I know, right? And now, because of those monsters, we don't have our bus tickets. And we were *so* looking forward to this tour."

The driver's eyebrows pinched together in concern. "Oh, bother. Hop aboard. We're heading to Briar's Hollow next. Home of the fairies!"

"I can't wait," CJ muttered sarcastically.

All the passengers stared at them as they climbed the stairs and made their way to the back of the bus. When they passed the couple CJ had seen on the street, CJ heard the wife whisper to her husband, "What are they wearing?"

The husband responded, "They're teenagers," as if that explained everything.

The girls found two empty seats in the last row and

both lunged for the window seat at the same time, trying to shove each other out of the way.

"Move!" Freddie whined. "I was here first."

"You were not!" CJ shot back.

Freddie grunted and managed to wedge her shoulder under CJ to push her back. CJ fell onto the floor with a plunk while Freddie happily climbed into the window seat with a gloating grin.

CJ sighed and surrendered into the aisle seat. There were two middle-aged ladies sitting in the opposite row who gaped at them like they were from another planet.

CJ reached into her backpack, grabbed one of the jelly doughnuts they'd stolen from the Auradon Prep kitchen, and discreetly squirted the red jelly onto the floor of the bus, creating what looked like a pool of blood.

"Oh, no," she said to the women across from her, faking concern. "I think someone is bleeding!"

The two women glanced at the floor and screamed, desperately looking around to find the source.

CJ sat back in her seat and snickered with satisfaction.

Freddie laughed, too, but then her expression grew serious. "Okay, that was kind of genius. But you really can't go around acting like that."

"Acting like what?"

"Like a"—Freddie lowered her voice to a whisper—"*VK.*"

"But I am a VK," CJ said, a bit too loudly. The women glanced at her, and CJ snapped at them with her teeth, causing them both to cower. "And so are you," she told Freddie. Then, under her breath, she added, "Although I shouldn't have to *remind* you of that."

"We need to try to blend in. How do you expect to find a fairy to help you if you keep acting like a brute?"

"Easy," CJ said breezily. "Take them hostage and *force* them to do it. That's what my dad always did."

"Uh-huh," Freddie said, crossing her arms. "And where is he now?"

CJ considered that for a moment, her body slouching in defeat. "Fine. Tell me what I need to do."

"You need to start acting like an AK."

CJ gagged. "And how do I do that?"

"Well, let's see. They make up a lot of words."

CJ perked up. "Like 'polite'?"

"No, that's a real word."

" 'Compassionate'?"

Freddie sighed. "Also a real word."

CJ twisted her mouth in thought. " 'Warmhearted'!" she said with sudden excitement. "That has *got* to be a fake word. I mean, it's such a contradiction. Hearts aren't *warm*." She snort-laughed.

Freddie closed her eyes as though trying to hold on to her last strands of patience. "I mean like 'fabulosity'! And 'selfie-rific'! And 'thrappy'!"

CJ frowned. "'Thrappy'?"

"It's a combination of thrilled and happy," Freddie explained. "You know, like *extra* happy."

"Yeah, I'm not saying that."

"Also," Freddie went on, "you have to try to be nicer to people. Tone down the angsty pirate thing. *Compliment* people. Be civil."

"That's another made-up one, right? 'Civil'? Let me guess. It's a combination of evil and—"

Freddie shook her head. "I know it stinks, but just try it. Compliment that woman next to you. Say something nice about her."

CJ rolled her eyes. This was pointless. She really didn't understand how it was going to help her get her ship.

Reluctantly, she turned to the woman next to her and looked her up and down, searching for something she could compliment.

"Hey," CJ said, gesturing to the woman's face,

"you've got really great nose hair. Nice and long. Have you ever thought about beading it?" She tugged on one of her beaded strands of golden-brown hair. "Like mine, see?"

The woman looked horrified, immediately touching her nose.

CJ nodded. "You're welcome." Then she turned her attention back to Freddie, who was slowly shaking her head.

CJ threw her hands in the air. "What?"

GANGWAY!

Ahoy, Briar's Hollow!

How long do we have to stay here?

The village of Briar's Hollow looked exactly the way CJ had expected it to look: sickeningly cheerful.

In the center was a cobblestone street with several small shops selling everything from bread to dresses to costume fairy wings. Tourists milled about among the townsfolk—all fairies—who were dressed in traditional "Good Fairy" garb, with layered dresses, capes, and pointy hats in a variety of colors.

On the outskirts of town were rows upon rows of cottage-style houses, each with a thatched roof, a single brick chimney, a stone path leading to the front door, and a wooden mill churning water over a small stream.

"Audrey said woodcutters' cottages became all the rage after it was discovered that Flora, Fauna, and Merryweather were hiding Briar Rose in one," Freddie explained as the bus pulled to a stop and the passengers started to disembark. "They've been springing up ever since. Exact replicas."

"More like *cookie* cutters' cottages," CJ mumbled.

"Okay," Freddie said once they had stepped off the bus. "We need to find a fairy who's gullible enough to help us."

"Or," CJ said thoughtfully, "we do it my way."

"We're not kidnapping anyone. It didn't work with Tiger Lily and it won't work here."

CJ crossed her arms. "Fine, what do you suggest?"

Freddie glanced around the bustling street, full of shops, and her eyes lit up suddenly. "There!" she said, pointing to one of the storefronts.

CJ read the sign over the small wooden door.

NOT YOUR FAIRY GODMOTHER'S

BEAUTY PARLOR

"A salon?" CJ asked in disbelief.

"We'll tell her we're from Auradon Prep and that we're here on a school assignment."

"But why a salon?" CJ asked.

Freddie flashed one of her wicked grins. "You'll see."

She grabbed CJ's hand and led her across the road to the shop. A small chime jingled when they pushed the door open and stepped inside. The salon was quaint and homey, with wood floors and a low ceiling. There was a long rectangular mirror hanging on the wall, and four salon chairs faced it. Two middle-aged fairies sat with their heads under dryers while an older fairy with large round glasses was getting her wet hair combed out by a beautician.

"I think I've decided to dye my hair pink," the fairy with glasses told the stylist. "Or maybe blue. No, definitely pink. Or blue. Hmmm. What do you think, dear?"

The beautician looked up when Freddie and CJ walked in. "Why don't you think on it?" she told the woman. "I'll be right back."

The beautician, who was also a fairy, approached Freddie and CJ with a beaming smile. CJ noticed she was dressed head to toe in orange, but she appeared to have taken the traditional Good Fairy look and . . . well, *updated* it a bit. She'd shortened the hem on her dress and added a colorful paint-splattered belt and orange leather boots. She'd also ditched the pointy hat in favor of a much more modern orange ball cap, which read TEAM PHILLIP.

"Well, hello there, dearies. What can I do for you?"

Freddie shoved CJ forward and announced, "She wants a makeover."

"What?" CJ whispered harshly, glaring at her friend. Freddie raised her eyebrows as if to say, *Just go with it.*

CJ gritted her teeth and flashed her very best AK smile. "It's true. I need a new look."

The fairy beautician glanced over her outfit and clucked. "I can't argue with you there! Come. Have a seat. I'm Peony." She tugged CJ by the hand and sat her down in the last salon chair. CJ stared at her scowling reflection in the mirror. She was going to make Freddie walk the plank for this.

"So," Peony said, shaking out CJ's long golden-brown ponytail and finger-combing the strands. She seemed to grimace every time she snagged one of CJ's many tangles. "Where are you dearies from?"

"Auradon Prep," Freddie replied. "We're students."

Peony's face brightened. "Oh, really! Isn't that grand? Auradon Prep."

"I hear King Ben is quite the looker," the older fairy with glasses said, cutting into the conversation. "Am I right?"

Freddie shot CJ a warning look, and CJ refreshed her fake smile. "Oh, you mean Benny Boo? Yup, he's a cutie-pie. But I'm pretty sure he's taken."

Peony laughed as she futzed with CJ's hair. "Maybe just a little off the bottom and some layers in the front." She held up one of the beaded strands with her fingertips like it was a snake she was afraid to touch. "And we'll do something about these . . . things. Way too *piratey* for my taste."

CJ clenched the armrests of the chair until her knuckles turned white. She watched in horror as Peony grabbed three kinds of scissors, two combs, and countless spray bottles and placed them on a nearby tray.

"So what brings you lovelies all the way out from Auradon City?" she asked.

CJ opened her mouth to say something but Freddie beat her to the punch. "We're here on a school assignment. We're studying the physics of fairies."

"Oh, be still, my magic wand," Peony said, placing a hand to her chest. "My heart's all aflutter! That's marvelous. Simply marvelous!"

Freddie winked conspiratorially at CJ, and then her lips fell into a perfect pout. "Yes, it was," she lamented, "at first. But actually, I think we're going to fail the class."

CJ immediately caught on to what Freddie was doing, and she had to admit she was impressed. It was a clever trick, and CJ was relieved to see Freddie back to her old wicked ways again. She'd been worried about her friend a lot lately.

Peony stopped fiddling with the items on her tray and turned to look at Freddie. "What's that, now, my dear?"

Freddie put her hand to her forehead, like she was a princess who'd just fainted. "We tried. I promise we did. But fairy physics is just *so* complicated."

"Oh, come now," Peony said, patting Freddie's hand. "Maybe I can help. I am, after all, a fairy." She glanced at herself in the mirror and flashed a beatific grin.

"I don't know," Freddie said doubtfully. "It's really advanced stuff."

The fairy clucked. "Nonsense! Nothing's too advanced for me."

"Well," Freddie went on, "we're trying to understand the dynamics of shrinking magic."

Peony picked up a comb and waved it toward

Freddie. "Shrinking magic! Easy-peasy! We learned that in preschool."

"Really?" Freddie asked. "Could you show us how it works?" She reached into the pocket of CJ's backpack and pulled out the map. "Like on this old piece of scrap paper?"

CJ's heart hammered. She was starting to get a very bad feeling about this. What if they'd misinterpreted the clue? What if the fairy shrunk her map and then couldn't *unshrink* it? What if—

But her panicked thoughts were cut short when the fairy said in a disappointed tone, "Oh, well, we're really not supposed to use magic anymore. Official proclamation from King Beast and all."

CJ couldn't help feeling a small twinge of relief. Maybe they should just leave and figure out another way to unlock the next section of the map. But Freddie was still fully vested in the charade.

"Oh. Right," Freddie said, wilting. "I understand. That's finesies. I guess we'll just fail the class. It was what we were expecting, anyway."

Peony bit her lip thoughtfully, then leaned in close so the other customers couldn't hear. "Well, maybe just a *little* magic would be all right," she whispered, her eyes darting anxiously around the shop. "But we'll have to go into the back room."

CJ, happy to get away from those scissors and combs, shot out of the chair like it was on fire.

"Just give me a moment to put this dye in," Peony told them, walking over to the older fairy with glasses. "Did you decide on a color?" Peony asked her.

The older fairy smiled. "Yes. I'd like to make it pink. No, make it blue. No, definitely pink. Well . . ."

"Pink it is!" Peony said before the older fairy could change her mind again. She turned toward CJ. "Will you be a deary and hand me the pink dye from the shelf in the back room?"

CJ stepped into the small storeroom in the back of the shop and scanned the shelves and cabinets, stocked with beauty supplies. She quickly found the shelf of dyes and read the labels. A mischievous smile crossed her face as she plucked a bottle and delivered it to Peony. "Here you go. One bottle of *pink* hair dye."

"Thank you!" Peony smiled and started dousing the older fairy's hair with the liquid. Once she was finished, she led Freddie and CJ into the back room and closed the door. Then, after glancing over both shoulders, she reached into the pocket of her dress and pulled out a long sparkly wand that seemed to drip glittery dust with every movement of her hand.

"Now, it's not Fairy Godmother's wand, by any means, but it'll do the trick," Peony said, giving her wand a few practice swings. "Where is that piece of paper?"

Freddie held up the yellowed page again, with the ink side facing her to hide the treasure map from Peony's view. CJ felt a knot form in her stomach as she stood next to Freddie. She couldn't believe they were doing this. Getting help from a pixie? What would her father say?

The fairy took a deep breath, and with a swift flick of her wrist, a stream of white sparkly light shot out the tip of her wand. CJ could barely track it as it flew across the small shop, heading right toward them.

She shut her eyes tight. She couldn't watch. If this ended badly, she didn't want to see it.

She felt a blast of something hit her in the chest, like a gust of warm wind, and her whole body started to tingle.

Then she heard a loud, booming voice. It sounded a lot like Peony's voice, but for some reason it seemed to be coming from far above her head. "Oh, dear. That was not supposed to happen."

CJ glanced up and saw a staggeringly *huge* pair of orange go-go boots stomping toward them, the ground shaking with each step. And that was when CJ also noticed the rest of their surroundings. The shelves and cabinets that only a second before had been normal-sized were now ginormous.

"Gulping guppies!" CJ exclaimed with a sudden realization. "She shrunk us!"

SHIVER ME TIMBERS!

So, this isn't good.

CJ couldn't believe it. That useless pixie had shrunk them!

She looked at Freddie, letting out a loud gasp when she noticed that Freddie was no longer holding the map. Panicked, she looked all around them, thinking maybe it had simply slipped from Freddie's hand, but it was nowhere to be seen.

"What did you do?" CJ roared.

Freddie, who looked just as stunned by their sudden change in size, took a step back, stammering. "I-I-I didn't do anything! It was the fairy! She must have made a mistake!"

CJ struggled to keep her temper in check, but it was too late. She simply couldn't keep herself reined in. Just as she'd seen her dad do so many times, she exploded. *"I told you never to trust a fairy!"*

Freddie looked conflicted. "I don't think she did it on purpose."

"Oh, wake up, Freddie, and smell the pixie dust. Of *course* she did it on purpose. She hornswoggled us like a pro. She *tricked* us. She probably shrunk us so she could run off with the map and find the treasure herself. She's been playing us since we walked in that door. And now it's all over. We'll never get the map back. We'll never find the treasure. I'll never get my ship!"

CJ felt hot, angry tears spring to her eyes. She blinked hard to keep them at bay.

Don't cry. Do not *cry.*

She'd taught herself to hold back tears when she was just a little girl. Her father hated crying children. He hated children in general, actually. Most of the time he just barely seemed to tolerate CJ.

She'd learned at a young age that the best way to keep yourself from crying was to yell instead. The frustration had to come out somehow, and the people in her family always seemed to respond better to yelling.

She opened her mouth to scream something else at Freddie, but before she could get another word out, the floor started to tremble violently beneath their feet again. Clouds of dust and debris sprung up from the ground, like rain falling in reverse. She glanced up and saw that Peony was walking around, her giant orange boots shaking the earth with each step.

CJ leapt back to avoid being squished to death. "Oh my my my my my," Peony lamented, her voice sounding like thunderclaps. "Where did they go? Did I make them disappear? This is bad. Very, very bad."

"Doubloons!" CJ swore. "What do we do now?"

Freddie bit her lip in concentration. "Um . . . um . . ."

"Think!" CJ commanded her.

"I am thinking!" Freddie shot back. "Oh! Ally from Auradon Prep told me a story once about her mother."

CJ stared at her in utter disbelief. "You want to talk about lame AK family stories at a time like this?"

Freddie ignored her. "She said that one time when her mother, Alice, was in Wonderland, she accidentally got shrunk from drinking a potion."

"We didn't drink a potion," CJ pointed out.

"Just listen!" Freddie snapped. CJ could tell the stress

of the situation was getting to her friend. While CJ had always had a short fuse, Freddie was usually calm. "The point is she found something in her pocket—a piece of mushroom—that made her big again."

CJ shot her a blank stare. "So?"

"So!" Freddie said, as though it were obvious. "Check your pockets! Maybe all AK clothes come with some kind of anti-shrinking mushrooms."

They both checked their pockets.

Nothing.

Why was CJ not surprised?

She watched panic spread over Freddie's face as Freddie tried to think of another plan. She must have come up short, because a second later, Freddie cupped her hands over her mouth and started yelling into the sky. *"Help! Down here! We're down here! You shrunk us!"*

"She can't hear you," CJ said miserably, plopping down onto her backside. "We're the size of ants."

She couldn't believe what was happening. She should *never* have listened to Freddie. She should never have invited Freddie to come along in the first place. She should have heeded her father's advice from the very beginning. Sidekicks were a waste of time. They only got you in trouble. They only screwed things up.

Did Mr. Smee ever actually *help* her father? No. He just bumbled around, making a mess of things.

CJ hung her head in defeat. It was time for her to admit it to herself: the treasure hunt was over. They were going to stay bugs forever—or at least until someone stepped on them, which probably wouldn't take long.

But then CJ noticed something beneath her.

She remembered that when she had walked in there, the floor of the salon had been wood—cracked wood that looked like it was ages old. This floor was different. It was kind of an off-white color. Almost yellow. And it wasn't made of wood.

She reached down and rubbed her fingertip over the surface.

It was kind of scratchy and rough, almost like it was made out of . . .

Old paper?

CJ shot up and starting walking in a slow circle, taking in the black ink drawings and letters beneath her feet that stretched out to the horizon.

"The map!" she exclaimed. They were standing on *top* of it.

CJ glanced around, trying to orient herself amid the

landscape. It was difficult, because everything was now enormous. One dot on the trail was bigger than she was. But after a moment, she realized they were right on top of Briar's Hollow, where the trail had ended.

But as she stared down at the massive dots, she noticed something strange. The dots *didn't* stop in Briar's Hollow, as she had once thought. They kept going. A new trail was stretched out in front of her. But these dots were different. They weren't gigantic like the others. They were normal-sized. Well, normal-sized to her, and she was miniature.

Curiously, she followed the dots with her eyes, and she let out a shriek when she saw something a few steps away.

There was *more* of the map.

There was a new section she definitely hadn't noticed before. She could see a forest leading to an area called South Riding, and another castle positioned on the east shore, which was called Towering Heights.

Has this been here the whole time, CJ thought, *and we just couldn't see it?*

Then she had a sudden realization and whispered, "The smudge of dirt!"

She remembered when Freddie had grabbed the map

from her earlier. CJ had believed Freddie had gotten it dirty.

But it wasn't dirt at all.

It was this.

It was another part of the map.

CJ thought about the second half of the clue that had appeared alongside the dotted trail leading to Briar's Hollow.

When magic shrinks the big to small,
You'll see the final clue of all.

You'll see the final clue of all.

It had been there since they'd gone to the Enchanted Lake. They just hadn't been able to see it before because they were too big!

Excitedly, she knelt down and traced her finger across the newly revealed area and the tiny dotted treasure trail that stretched across it. But she stopped abruptly when her eyes fell upon the northernmost tip—upon a small island that seemed to rise from the ink-black sea like a drowned ship resurfacing.

Her heart pounded. Her breath hitched. Her entire body went numb.

"Freddie!" CJ turned to see her friend struggling to push against a giant wooden pole that was as thick as a tree trunk. She peered up to see that it was the handle of a broom.

"One second," Freddie said with a grunt, "I've almost got it." She backed up a few paces and ran, hurling herself against the wooden stick. It didn't budge. But Freddie was thrown back from the impact. "Ow!" she cried, holding her shoulder.

"What are you doing?" CJ asked.

"Trying to knock over this broom to get the fairy's attention."

"Come look at this!"

Rubbing her wounded arm, Freddie made her way to CJ and let out a shriek of her own when she saw what CJ had discovered.

"What is that?" Freddie asked, her eyes wide.

"It's the last section of the map! It's been here the whole time."

"You mean," Freddie began, seemingly putting the pieces together, "Peony was *supposed* to shrink us instead of the map?"

CJ nodded. "Apparently so."

"But how do you know it's the *last* section of the map?"

CJ grinned, letting the delicious sense of victory wash over her. It was just as sweet as she'd always imagined. "Because of *that*." She pointed to the top of the new section, and Freddie's eyes tracked her finger.

The dotted trail extended off the east coast of Auradon, crossed a small sea labeled HOOK'S BAY, curved around a large landmass called Never Land, and stopped just to the north, at a small island that resembled a skull rising from the water.

The words written below the island were familiar to CJ, because she'd heard them in many stories of her father's adventures.

And now, marked with two slanted lines crossing in the middle, those words were leading her to the beginning of her *own* adventure.

SKULL ROCK.

X MARKS THE SPOT

Holy mackerel.

Things are getting good.

"One . . . two . . . *three*!" CJ and Freddie slammed against the broomstick with all their might.

The broom gave way. Freddie held CJ back as it wobbled and then finally tipped over.

"Oh, my!" screamed Peony, who had been pacing the floor, trying to figure out how to make Freddie and CJ reappear.

Peony glanced at the broom on the ground.

"C'mon!" Freddie called. She leapt onto the broomstick and began jumping up and down. CJ reluctantly joined her, even though she felt ridiculous.

But she was too close to lose it all now. She had unlocked the map, followed the clues, and found the location of the buried treasure. She was so close to buying her pirate ship and setting off on her first big adventure she could taste it.

Of course her treasure would be on Skull Rock. It made so much sense. It was almost poetic. Her father had always said that Skull Rock was one of the few places in Never Land that a pirate could call home.

And that was where she was heading.

She jumped up and down on the broomstick—which might as well have been a log, as thick as it seemed—and flailed her arms in the air, screaming at the top of her lungs. "Down here, you stupid pixie! We're down here!"

CJ saw the fairy squint and bend down to get a closer look.

"Well, turn my raven to stone, look at that!" She dropped to her knees, causing a trembling in the ground that nearly knocked both CJ and Freddie off the broom. "Oh, my, silly me, I must have shrunk *them* instead of the paper."

"About time she figured it out," CJ muttered.

The fairy cocked her wand back and gave it a flick.

Giant sparks of white light rained down on them, and then . . . presto!

CJ and Freddie were normal-sized again.

Oh, thank badness, CJ thought.

"There," Peony said, stashing her wand back in her pocket. "Much better. Sorry about the mix-up."

CJ lunged for the map, which was still on the floor, and hastily rolled it up. As she did, she noticed that the new section—the part leading her to Skull Rock— looked like a smudge of dirt again.

Whoever had hidden the treasure and enchanted the map had obviously wanted to make sure that no one could find the final location unless they were incredibly small.

Like *pixie dust* small.

CJ stuffed the map into her pocket and threw her backpack on. "Well, thanks for shrinking us. And, you know, unshrinking us. We'd best be going now."

She grabbed Freddie by her kimono sleeves and pulled her back into the salon, just in time to hear the older fairy with the glasses scream in horror at her reflection: "My hair! It's black as a raven!"

Freddie looked at CJ, who shrugged innocently and hurried out of the shop.

"Wait!" Peony called after them. "What about your makeover?"

But CJ was already closing the door behind them with a jingle.

Once they were safe on the street, CJ immediately tied her hair back into its usual billowing ponytail. "Ah, much better."

"Oh, no!" Freddie cried out, pointing up the road.

CJ turned around. "What?"

"Our bus is gone!"

But CJ was completely unfazed. "We don't *need* a bus to get where we're going," she told Freddie. "We need a *boat*. Skull Rock is an *island*, remember?"

"A boat?" Freddie repeated skeptically. "But how are we going to get a boat?"

CJ was two steps ahead of her. She'd already asked herself that very question *and* come up with a solution. "Easy. We'll just find a ship captain and take him hostage."

Freddie shook her head. "For the last time, we're not taking anyone hostage."

CJ crossed her arms. "Do you have a better idea?"

Freddie thought for a moment. "My dad always told me stories about the Bayou d'Orleans. They have lots of boats there, so why don't we just steal one?"

A wicked grin spread across CJ's face. She was glad to see that Freddie was back to her usual evil self. CJ clapped Freddie on the back. "Good thinking! So how do we get to the bayou?"

But Freddie didn't respond, and a moment later CJ noticed that Freddie's face had gone deathly pale. And her eyes were so wide they looked like full moons.

"Okay, don't panic," Freddie said in an anxious tone. "Don't panic."

CJ was confused. "Why would I panic?"

"I was talking to myself!" Freddie snapped. Then she hastily grabbed CJ by the arm and pulled her behind an idling delivery truck parked on the street.

"What's going on?" CJ asked.

"Look out there," Freddie muttered between clenched teeth.

CJ peered out from behind the truck, her eyes scanning the street until she found the source of Freddie's sudden anxiety.

On the sidewalk, making her way straight toward them, was the pink-clad, high-heeled, headbanded, prissy princess Audrey.

BLIMEY!

We gotta split.

And fast.

"We need to get out of here," Freddie said, "and without her seeing us."

"So what if she sees us?" CJ asked, peeking from behind the truck. "What's the big deal?"

What did CJ care if one of the AKs spotted them? Let them try to catch her and send her back to the isle. She had the last piece of the map. She was golden.

Pun intended.

"What's the big deal?" Freddie repeated, clearly losing her patience. "The big deal is she could tell on us.

She could report us to Headmistress Fairy Godmother. She could have us expelled from Auradon Prep."

"*You* expelled," CJ corrected spitefully. "She could have *you* expelled. Remember, I'm not a student there. I could care less what Audrey or any other lame AK thinks."

"Me too. Trust me. But I don't want to get the boot when we're this close to your pirate's booty."

CJ smiled. "Now there's the wicked VK that I know and hate. So we need to figure out how to get to the bayou and—"

But CJ's words were cut short when the truck they were hiding behind rumbled to life and they heard someone—presumably the driver—say, "See you next week!"

Freddie's eyes widened in panic. Their cover—it was leaving. In just a few seconds they would be exposed, standing in the middle of the street with nothing to block them from Audrey's view.

Freddie and CJ both spun around to look at the truck. It was the first time either of them had taken notice of what was written on the side of it. They read the words at the same time, then turned toward each other to share a look of disbelief.

"C'mon!" CJ said, grabbing Freddie by the hand. They ran to the back of the truck. CJ struggled to unlatch the loading door while Freddie kept glancing over her shoulder at the place where they'd last seen Audrey.

When CJ finally managed to swing the door open, she hopped inside and called for Freddie. "Get in!" she commanded.

But Freddie was turned away from her, and she seemed to be frozen to her spot. CJ followed her gaze and understood what was happening. Audrey had stopped in the middle of the street and was staring in their direction, her head cocked to the side and her eyes squinting at them, like she was trying to figure out why they looked so familiar.

They were still in their AK costumes, which were undoubtedly throwing her off.

"Freddie!" CJ whispered. "Get in the truck!"

But Freddie didn't move.

Audrey took a curious step forward, looking suspicious. "Freddie?" she asked. "Is that you?"

Freddie visibly flinched.

The truck lurched as the driver threw it into gear, readying to pull away. "Freddie!" CJ said a little louder. "The truck is leaving!"

And just as she said it, she felt the vibration under her feet. She looked down to see the cobblestone street moving as the truck slowly pulled away from the curb.

"Freddie!" CJ yelled, no longer caring who heard.

Audrey heard. Her gaze traveled to the back of the truck, where CJ was still standing with the loading door wide open.

"Freddie!" Audrey echoed with annoyance as she stomped toward the truck. "What are you doing here? Why aren't you at school? If you left without Headmistress's permission, I could seriously get you in trouble."

That seemed to do the trick. Freddie unfroze and turned around to see the empty street behind her. Her eyes shot up the road at the disappearing truck, and she started to run.

The truck was gaining speed, though, and CJ feared her friend wouldn't make it. "C'mon!" she urged Freddie, who was trying to run as best she could in her floral kimono.

CJ grabbed on to a strap attached to the wall and

reached out her hand. Freddie tried to grab it, but she couldn't reach, and the truck was quickly moving farther away.

CJ studied the strap in her hand. It looked just like a ship's lanyard. That gave her an idea. She wrapped the strap around her wrist twice, backed up, and took a running leap. She swung in a wide arc behind the truck and reached out her hand to Freddie. Freddie caught it just in time and jumped, and they both swung back into the moving truck, crashing into a crate of food, as the driver rounded the corner and headed out of town.

CJ pulled the giant loading door closed and collapsed against the wall. "What were you thinking?" she asked breathlessly. "Why were you just standing there?"

Freddie didn't reply. She sat on the floor, quietly staring down at her hands. She appeared to be deep in thought.

"Freddie," CJ said, prompting her.

Still her friend remained silent. Then, after a few long moments, Freddie whispered, "She's going to tell on me. She's going to report me to Headmistress."

That's why she's so upset?

CJ snorted. "So what?"

Freddie continued to stare at her hands.

CJ huffed. "I don't understand why you even care. You're a VK. Like me. You're not supposed to like it there."

"But I do!" Freddie cried in a sudden outburst that made CJ flinch. "I do like it there! Okay? I'm sorry if that doesn't fit into your big plans for world domination, but I like it at Auradon Prep. I have fun there. People sing there. *I* get to sing there."

CJ sighed.

"And we get dressed up for things," Freddie went on, as though she hadn't even heard her. "And we drink tea. And"—Freddie's voice became quiet—"I'm seen as more than just Dr. Facilier's daughter."

CJ guffawed. "Oh, wake up and smell the fish oil! Nobody there sees you as anything more than Dr. Facilier's daughter. Everywhere you go there, that's all they see. The daughter of a villain. The daughter of their enemy."

Freddie shook her head. "That's where you're wrong. Yeah, maybe at first they did, but I don't know. . . . The last few days, it started to feel like they were coming around, seeing me as a person. My own person."

CJ rolled her eyes and shook her head. "You're fooling yourself if you think those people care about you."

"They care about me more than *anyone* on the island ever did. Including my own parents!"

"This is why we're here!" CJ thundered, gesturing to the inside of the truck. "That's why we got *off* the island. So we could go on our *own* adventure. So we could leave them all behind."

"This was never *my* adventure," Freddie reminded her. "I'm only here to help you, remember? After we find the treasure, I'm going back to Auradon Prep."

"Fine!" CJ shouted. "If that's what you want, then go! Why wait until *after* we find the treasure? Just go now! If you want to give up a life of *real* fun, of *real* adventure, for a bunch of singing princesses and chocolate fountains, be my guest. My father was right. Sidekicks are a waste of time. I can do this on my own. I never needed you to begin with. I never needed anyone!"

"Fine!" Freddie echoed. "Go steal your boat and find your stupid treasure. You're just like your father! He was so obsessed with finding Peter Pan he nearly lost his entire crew. And now you've become so obsessed with this map and that treasure, you're going to lose the only friend you have left."

"You're not my friend," CJ spat. "You're an AK. I'm not friends with AKs."

CJ immediately saw hurt flash in Freddie's eyes. She tamped down the guilt that threatened to bubble up inside her.

Good, she told herself. *She should be upset. She should realize that deserting me for a bunch of prissy princesses is a mistake.*

Freddie looked like she was about to say something else, but just then the truck lurched, causing both girls to lose their balance. CJ clung to a nearby rack to steady herself while Freddie clung to the door handle. Then they just stood there, glaring at each other, stewing in their mutual anger.

The truck stopped, and a moment later the loading door popped open, breaking both of them from their trances. The driver startled at the sight of them. "What are you two doing back here?" he asked.

"*I* was just leaving," CJ replied, casting a spiteful look in Freddie's direction. She grabbed her backpack and hopped off the truck. "I have a boat to catch."

ÆNCHORS ÆWEIGH!

*Forget Freddie. I never needed
a sidekick, anyway.*

#ByeFacilier

The Bayou d'Orleans was a happening place.

The streets were alive with activity: jazz clubs bursting with the sounds of soulful grooves, restaurants pumping out delicious scents of boiling seafood, and people dancing in the streets. The sun was already starting to set and the town was lighting up with excitement. The general joyfulness in the air made CJ grit her teeth.

What do these people have to be so happy about?

She pulled her red pirate coat tight around her, trying to block out the gleeful energy hitting her from all sides. She'd finally ditched that stupid AK costume, almost immediately after jumping out of the delivery truck. It felt so good to peel off the clothes that represented everything she hated and stuff them into a trash can, where they belonged.

As CJ neared the docks, she could smell the salty sea air. She breathed it in, relishing it. This was the smell of a pirate's life. And a pirate's life was *definitely* for her.

She closed her eyes and inhaled deeply, waiting for the comforting scent to calm her heart, which was still pounding from her fight with Freddie. But it was another scent in the air that stopped CJ in her tracks.

She opened her eyes and peered around her, searching for the source.

What was that?

It was sweet and it made CJ's mouth water.

Her eyes fell on a small club right across from the bayou's marina. It was lit up like the rest of the stores in town. A neon sign hung just above the entrance.

BASS NOTES AND BEIGNETS

CJ's mind grudgingly flashed back to the conversation she'd had with Freddie on the bridge as they'd traveled to the Enchanted Lake. Freddie was talking about those stupid beignets and the stories her father used to tell her about them.

Then she remembered what had happened next: how they'd dove into the Enchanted Lake, thinking it would unlock the map; how they'd splashed each other and Freddie had slipped and face-planted right into the water.

CJ caught herself smiling at the memory and quickly erased the grin from her face.

Stupid Freddie. Stupid lake. Stupid beignets.

CJ snorted and kept walking, doing her best to breathe through her mouth. The dock was calling to her. The treasure was calling to her. It had been calling to her since she was a little girl, and now it was so close she could practically feel all that gold and silver.

She would *not* veer off course.

When she reached the marina, she immediately laid eyes on a small rowboat that was tied up to one of the docks, completely unattended. It wasn't the luxurious pirate ship she'd always dreamed about, but that would come later, once she'd found the treasure and could finally set off on her epic grand adventure.

Even though the boat reminded her of the kind Mr. Smee used to row her father around in, it would have to do. According to the treasure map, Never Land and Skull Rock were north of the bayou. All she had to do was sail east out of the harbor, turn north once she spotted the peninsula of Towering Heights, and keep rowing until she reached Never Land. Then Skull Rock was just around the corner.

But suddenly the thought of navigating the open water in a rowboat without even a compass to guide her made her stomach contract. Once she got out there, how would she know which way was north? What if she got turned around? What if she steered the boat the wrong way and ended up back on the Isle of the Lost?

No, she assured herself. *You'll be fine. You don't need a compass. You have pirate's blood. Never Land is where your father is from. It will call to you. It will guide you home.*

With a deep breath, she untied the boat and used her foot to push back from the dock, feeling a strange anticipation travel through her as she watched the harbor grow fainter and fainter in the distance.

This was it! She was doing it! She was in a boat. In

open water. All those years spent staring at maps and pictures and dreaming of oceans and far-off lands, and now she was finally there.

With a contended sigh, CJ sat down on her little wooden bench and began to row out to sea.

SKELETON CREW

Boat.

Party of one.

With every stroke of the oars, the city of Bayou d'Orleans became smaller and smaller.

Soon the lights of the cafés and clubs and stores looked like twinkling stars on the horizon. CJ's arms were already sore and she was starting to feel winded, but she pressed on, keeping a clear picture of the treasure in her mind as she rowed. Gold and silver and precious gems. Enough for her to buy a fleet of ships if she wanted.

But every time CJ tried to visualize herself unearthing the heavy wooden box and creaking open the lid, she couldn't help imagining Freddie sitting next to her. She couldn't help hearing Freddie's silky laugh as riches beyond their wildest dreams spilled out around them. She couldn't help seeing Freddie's mischievous smile at knowing they had succeeded. *Together.*

Freddie was probably halfway back to her precious Auradon Prep by then.

CJ tried to shake the imagery from her head. It was ridiculous to think like that. After all, in every dream she'd had of that day, there had never been anyone with her. In her fantasies, she was always by herself, a lone pirate finally uncovering her treasure.

Freddie had just been . . .

What?

A helper?

A sidekick?

A first mate?

No, CJ thought with a sudden overwhelming sadness.

Freddie had been her partner—a *true* partner. She was helpful and innovative and smart. She was cunning and devious and shrewd. She kept CJ in line and made sure they didn't get caught. She had been a true friend.

But mostly, CJ realized as a single tear sprung to her

eye, Freddie had been *fun*. She'd made the whole journey worthwhile. She'd turned it into . . .

An adventure.

The thought struck CJ like a lightning bolt.

All her life, CJ had thought she needed a ship and a pile of gold to have a proper adventure. Yet wasn't that what she and Freddie had been doing the whole time? Swimming in enchanted lakes, dressing up in silly disguises, infiltrating villages, tricking locals, getting shrunk by fairy magic, stowing away in delivery vans . . .

What were all those things if not adventures in and of themselves?

With a huff, CJ dug her left oar into the water and spun the boat around. She might have started this thing alone, but she wasn't going to finish it alone. This victory was for both of them.

It was time to get her friend back.

SECOND-IN-COMMAND

I miss Freddie.

Who would've thunk?

The whole way back to the bayou, CJ thought about where Freddie might be.

Is she already back at the school?

Will I have to find another delivery truck or tour bus heading to Auradon Prep?

But when CJ pulled her tiny rowboat up to the dock and spotted the Bass Notes and Beignets jazz club in the distance, she knew exactly where her friend would be.

As soon as she set foot inside the club, she was

overwhelmed by the delicious scents wafting from the kitchen. The sweetness in the air practically danced on her tongue.

CJ scanned the room, holding her breath. She spotted a small table in the corner, but she couldn't see the person sitting at it, because there was a plate piled so high with sugar-coated beignets they completely blocked her view. But then CJ caught sight of a tiny purple top hat poking above the stack of pastries, and she let out a deep sigh of relief.

As CJ approached, she saw that Freddie was sitting alone, absentmindedly stuffing fried dough into her mouth as she watched a sultry lounge singer perform on a small stage. The singer was dressed in a long sequined red gown and a matching feathered headband. She was accompanied by a trio of musicians, but no one except Freddie was listening to them. The woman's voice was simply mesmerizing—silky and smooth—and for a moment, CJ forgot why she'd gone into the club; she was so entranced by the sound. At least, she did until Freddie called her name.

CJ blinked and turned to her friend, giving an awkward little wave. "Hi, Freddsie," she said, her usual pirate flair gone from her voice. She was quiet and vulnerable now. And she hated it. She cleared her throat and motioned toward the front door. "Can we talk?"

Freddie was reluctant to leave. It was obvious she was really enjoying the singer, but she finally stood up and followed CJ toward the door, stopping at the last minute to run back and grab her plate of beignets.

"I thought you'd be halfway to Skull Rock by now," Freddie said bitterly as they stood outside on the street.

"I was." CJ paused and looked at the ground. "I came back."

Freddie's surprise was written all over her face. "Why?"

"Because . . ." CJ began hesitantly as a hundred lies flooded her mind at once.

Because I need your help with directions.

Because my arms got tired and I need someone else to row the boat.

Because the treasure is bound to be too heavy for just one person to carry.

But she couldn't say any of those things. She couldn't lie to her friend. It was time to tell Freddie the truth. It had been there all along; CJ had just been too blind and stubborn and *Hookish* to see it.

"Because I missed you!" She let the words tumble out of her mouth.

Freddie looked skeptical. "What? You missed having someone to order around?"

"No," CJ said, and then stopped to think. "Well, yeah, a little, but that's not it. I missed you just being there. It didn't feel right without you. It felt empty. Like something was missing."

Freddie's fingers fidgeted against the edge of the plate. She looked anxious and doubtful, like she was trying to figure out whether to believe CJ.

"It's not fun without you," CJ went on. "It's not a real *adventure* without you."

Freddie was silent for a long time, and CJ was starting to get nervous. What if her friend wouldn't forgive her? What if she'd messed up too badly to make it right this time? What if—

"I had fun, too," Freddie admitted softly. "Even though you can be difficult and stubborn and obsessive."

CJ felt her emotions get riled up again, but she pushed them down and instead cocked an eyebrow and flashed her signature pirate grin. "What can I say? Obsessiveness runs in the family."

Freddie laughed. "I guess I shouldn't be too quick

to judge. It's not like my father passed down a bunch of admirable traits to me, either." She peered down at her plate. "Apart from our impeccable taste in food."

CJ laughed, too, and grabbed a beignet from the plate. The smell had been driving her bonkers. She stuffed the whole thing into her mouth, not quite sure what to expect.

It was positively sinful. The flavor of the sweet sugar mixed with the slightly salty dough was the most delicious thing she'd ever tasted. Her eyes rolled back in her head and her body slumped a little. "Mmm. This is amazing."

CJ immediately reached for another, but Freddie moved the plate away. "Hey! Get your own."

CJ chuckled and sprayed powdered sugar all over her friend's face.

Freddie gasped, stuffed a beignet into her own mouth, and huffed a sugary white cloud at CJ. This went on, back and forth, until the plate was empty and they were both laughing uncontrollably, their faces covered in sugar.

"C'mon," CJ said, linking her arm through Freddie's and guiding her toward the marina, where her stolen boat was docked. "We have a buried treasure to dig up."

SKULL AND CROSSBONES

Land ho!

Or skull ho?

CJ and Freddie took turns rowing, but they seemed to have been traveling forever and there was still no land in sight. Never Land and Skull Rock were a lot farther away than they'd looked on CJ's treasure map.

After what felt like days at sea, CJ dropped her oar and pointed into the distance.

Towering above their little boat, like a mighty shark emerging from the water, was Skull Rock, her father's home away from home.

CJ could have sworn she heard it whispering to her, "Welcome back, Hook."

It was just as her father had always described in his stories. An island made entirely out of stone, in the shape of a giant human skull that seemed to be floating in the middle of the sea, water lapping between its teeth, birds circling its cheekbones.

It was a terrifying sight to behold. Even for two villain kids.

They had grown up on an island marred by evil and corruption and sin. Yet with the empty darkness that loomed in the skull's eyes, the deep black water that surrounded them, and the birds cawing ominously overhead like a warning signal, *this* might have been the scariest thing CJ had ever seen.

There was no shore to anchor the boat. No sand. No dock. The only entrance was through the cavernous hollow of the skull's mouth. But the tide was rising quickly. CJ could feel it lifting the boat with every gentle sway of the water. Soon the mouth of the skull would be completely buried under the water and there would be no way in.

It was now or never.

CJ shuddered as she steered the boat through the

jaws of the skull and the girls found themselves in a dark, echoing cavern, surrounded by nothing but damp rock.

"What now?" Freddie asked, shivering.

CJ didn't know. The map had only specified that they needed to go to Skull Rock and that the treasure was somewhere in there; it gave no indication of how to—

CJ's thoughts were cut short when she spotted something on the wall of the cave. It looked like a ladder carved into the rocks. She followed it with her eyes, higher and higher and higher, until it finally ended at the far edge of the large gaping hole that formed the skull's left eye.

"I think . . ." CJ said, trying to keep her voice from shaking. "I think I'm supposed to climb up there."

Freddie followed her gaze. "Are you sure?"

CJ shook her head. "No. But I don't see any other options."

"Should I come with you?" Freddie asked, and CJ sensed the fear in her voice. She was trying not to show it, just as CJ was. Just like all VKs were taught to do on the Isle of the Lost.

But CJ had never felt more terrified in all her life. And she wasn't sure she was going to be able to hide it this time.

"No," she said. "The tide is rising fast. You stay here and make sure the boat doesn't get lost. We'll need a way to get out of here with the treasure if I find it." She stopped, then corrected herself. "*When* I find it."

"Okay," Freddie said, but she sounded about as certain of the plan as CJ felt. "Be careful."

CJ nodded. "I will." Then she stepped off the boat onto a nearby rock and headed toward the ladder.

"Wait!" Freddie called out. She pulled something from her pocket and tossed it at CJ, who caught the object in her hand and studied it.

It was a pack of matches. She flipped it over and saw the logo of Bass Notes and Beignets on the back side.

"I took it from the jazz club," Freddie said, "so I could remember the name if I ever went back to the bayou." She nodded toward the skull's black-as-night left eye. "It looks pretty dark up there. You might need a little light."

"Thanks," CJ said, feeling a swell of gratitude rise in her chest.

She positioned her hands on the ladder carved into the rock and, with a deep breath, started to climb.

HEAVE HO!

Treasure, here I come!

This isn't so bad. As long as I don't fall.
That might be bad.

Ascending the rock ladder was easy for CJ. She was good at climbing. She and Freddie used to climb all the time back on the Isle of the Lost when they were kids. Not rocks or trees or anything, but garbage heaps and collapsed building rubble.

When she reached the top of the ladder, she turned around to wave at Freddie, who looked incredibly small from way up there. CJ thought she must be at least thirty feet high.

I made it, she thought with relief.

Then she turned back and saw the inside of the skull's eye for the first time.

CJ gulped.

It had no bottom. She had expected there to be a floor she could walk on, but instead there was a long, gaping hole that stretched across the entire length of the eye. And it was so dark down there she couldn't see anything. But she could *hear* something. It sounded like waves, rough and violent, slamming repeatedly against a stone wall.

In other words, she shouldn't fall down there.

She glanced across to the other side, where the skull's nose would have been, and saw a sliver of light, like a beacon calling to her. She was pretty sure she was supposed to get across the giant chasm.

But how?

It was way too far to jump. And she couldn't scurry around the edge of it. The stone there was too thin.

Think, she commanded herself. *You're the daughter of the greatest pirate ever to sail the seven seas. You can do this.*

Then she looked up and her stomach flipped. Hanging from the ceiling of the cave was a line of insanely sharp steel hooks, ten of them, spaced about three feet apart.

She shivered at the sight. The hooks were nearly identical to the one her father had on his left hand.

She instantly knew what she had to do. She had to swing across, using the steel hooks as handles. And she had to do it without impaling her hand. If she grabbed a hook the wrong way, it would damage her hand at best, and at worst cause her to plummet to her death.

But CJ felt confident. After all, she'd been avoiding getting accidentally stabbed by her father's fake hand her entire life. And with all the flailing about he did when he lost his temper (which was pretty much daily), it wasn't always easy.

CJ sucked in a deep breath, crept to the edge of the ravine, and reached for the first handle. She was lucky her hands were small. They fit nicely in the curved *non-*sharp part of the hook. She used her feet to kick off the rock, gliding smoothly to the next handle. She caught it without a problem.

She knew she had to keep up her momentum if she was going to make it all the way across. If she paused and let herself swing to a stop, it would be much harder to get started again. So she trusted her instincts and immediately released the first hook, letting the momentum from her original jump push her to the next one.

After a few seconds, CJ was really getting the hang of it. She kept her body agile as she soared effortlessly through the air from hook to hook.

This is easy, CJ thought. *Almost fun.*

But just as she was grabbing the second-to-last hook, she heard something below her—a strange sound that echoed ominously against the stone walls of the chamber.

CJ froze, her arms stretched overhead, both hands still gripping a hook as she swayed to a stop over the dark ravine below.

What is that noise? she thought.

It was repetitive. Almost rhythmic. But before she could identify what it was, her left eyebrow started to twitch.

That's weird. Why is my eyebrow twitching?

The sound got louder. Her eyebrow twitched again. She felt the urge to rub it, but her hands were occupied at the moment. And was it just her imagination or was her eyebrow moving in *tempo* with the noise?

Pshh. She pushed the thought away. That would

be impossible. She'd never heard of a face twitching in rhythm, except for when her father—

Her thoughts were cut short as the noise got louder and finally became recognizable.

Tick. Tock. Tick. Tock.

Fear seized her body. She tried to peer down into the pit, but it was pitch-black. She could only hear that horrific sound. It seemed like it was getting closer.

Tick. Tock. Tick. Tock.

It was definitely a ticking clock. Ever since she was a child, her father had instilled a debilitating fear of ticking clocks in her. But why would there be a ticking clock at the bottom of the cave?

The answer came to her a second later, and she screamed and flailed her legs in panic.

Tick. Tock!

The Crocodile that had eaten her father's hand! He was down there! He had to be. That vicious beast had pursued Captain Hook all over Never Land. CJ's father always told her that the Crocodile could smell him, as if he had gotten a taste for his blood when he ate the hand and had been hungry for the rest of him ever since.

He must smell me, too! CJ thought with horror. *I have the same blood!*

She had to get out of there, and fast.

She couldn't see down into the ravine, so she didn't know how high the water was, but she knew the tide was rising fast.

How long before he can reach me? Can crocodiles climb walls?

CJ didn't want to wait around to find out. She was only one hook away from the safety of the ledge. She launched her body forward, reaching for the last rung. But because she was starting from a stop, she didn't have enough momentum, and her hand grappled for the hook and missed. And before she could even realize what had happened, her other hand released the second-to-last rung.

Then CJ was falling.

HOOKED!

Well, it's been fun.

I'm about to feed the fish . . .
or, rather, the crocodile.

CJ's scream echoed throughout all of Skull Rock.

She was pretty sure that was it. That would be the end of her. But then, suddenly, her body was jerked upward with such ferocity the scream was choked off. Now she was just dangling there, confused.

She peered up to see that the final hook had gotten caught on the sleeve of her pirate coat and was keeping her suspended above the deep chasm.

She breathed out a sigh of relief. She was saved!

But not for long. Because a millisecond later, she

heard the distinct sound of ripping. She glanced up again and another wave of panic shot through her. *The fabric!* It was tearing. The hook was going to rip right through it.

Tick. Tock. Tick. Tock.

The sound of the ticking clock seemed to be getting closer by the second.

She reached up and tried to grab the hook with her dangling hand, but it was too far away and the twisting motion seemed to rip the sleeve faster.

Anxiously, CJ looked around and saw the ledge of the ravine only a few feet in front of her. She just needed to build up enough momentum to swing herself onto it—before the hook ripped clean through her coat and she plummeted to her death.

No pressure.

She started to slowly sway her body back and forth. But with each pump of her legs, she felt the fabric tear and she dropped an inch closer to her untimely demise.

CJ drew in a breath. It was now or never.

With one violent jolt, she swung herself toward the rocky ledge just as the fabric gave way and she started to fall again. She arched her body, bending her back and reaching out with her toes.

Her feet managed to find the rock, but her upper body was still far behind. She nearly toppled backward. With an *"oomph"* she flung herself forward with all her might and landed face-first on the stone floor.

Her cheek stung. Her head throbbed from the impact. But she was alive. She had made it.

She jumped to her feet and let out a triumphant whoop. That was when she noticed that her left hand felt a lot heavier than her right. She glanced down at the sleeve of her coat to see the hook still impaled in the fabric.

It hadn't ripped through after all. The hook had simply come loose.

She carefully removed it from her sleeve and placed it in her pocket. Her father would be the first person to tell you that a hook could make a very good weapon in a pinch.

Steeling herself, CJ inched forward, crossing over the bridge of the skull's nose. But the path in front of her was dark. She found the matches Freddie had given her and lit one. It provided enough light to see where she was walking. She was in a dark, narrow passageway with a low ceiling. CJ had to duck to avoid bumping her head.

She kept her eyes open and her senses on high alert.

She had no idea what was coming next, or whether the whole thing had just been one giant trap and she was walking straight to her grave.

When the match burned down to the end, she dropped it and lit another. She didn't even see the hole in front of her until she took another step and didn't feel the ground.

She lost her balance and fell backward onto the cold, damp stone. She held out her match and crawled slowly forward, thinking she'd nearly tripped on a pothole.

But this was no pothole.

This was a deep, dark pit. She waved her match inside, but the measly light only managed to illuminate a few feet below. The pit seemed to be bottomless.

It's the other eye of the skull, CJ thought, and a shiver ran through her. But it wasn't her usual fear. It was something else. Like a hunch. A warning bell. It was almost as though the blood in her veins was singing, crooning out a dark pirate song.

There was something down there in that pit.

She could hear it calling to her.

Just before her match burned out, she noticed a rope hanging from the ceiling. It traveled right down into the center of the pit.

A rope! Hallelujah!

She reached out and gave the rope a firm tug. She couldn't see where it was attached, but it was clearly secure. With one foot wrapped around the rope and the other still safe on the ground, she tested her weight.

It held.

She released the other foot and slowly started to lower herself into the dark pit. After she'd been descending for what felt like forever, she decided to have another look.

She held on to the rope with one hand while the other lit a match. She swung it around her, left, right, up, and . . .

A scream instantly rose in her throat and she had to clamp her mouth shut and bite her lip to keep it from escaping. She could see the bottom of the pit now. She was nearly there.

In the center she could make out the unmistakable shape of a wooden treasure chest. *Her* treasure chest— the one she'd been dreaming about her entire life. The one she'd tracked across the Auradon countryside. She'd finally found it.

There was only one problem.

It was surrounded by a dozen sleeping crocodiles.

CLEAR THE DECK!

Oh, I am so out of here. . . .

CJ immediately started to scramble back up the rope.

There was no way she was going down into that pit with a bunch of hungry crocodiles that had a taste for Hook family blood.

It was hopeless. A lost cause. Whoever had hidden the treasure down there had obviously been trying to keep her father, and any of his descendants, away from it. Everything she'd encountered thus far—fairies, ticking clocks, crocodiles—seemed like deliberate reminders of her father's past. Not to mention the map was completely useless on the Isle of the Lost, where her father was still trapped. It was as though whoever had enchanted it wanted to make sure Captain Hook could never unlock it, could never find the treasure.

But I found it, CJ thought. *It's right down there.*

CJ stopped climbing. The rope swung back and forth slightly as she hung there, letting the thought echo in her mind.

Ever since she was a little girl, she'd wanted to prove her worth. She'd wanted to show her father that she could be just as cunning and conniving and swashbuckling as he was. She wanted to prove that she wasn't just a pirate's *daughter.* She was a pirate in her own right.

If she turned around now, she would never get her ship. She would never set off on her epic adventure. She would never prove herself worthy of the name Hook.

She was so close. She couldn't quit now.

Besides, whoever had hidden the treasure way down there, surrounded by bloodthirsty crocodiles, had *expected* whoever found it to do just that: to quit. To flee. To fail. And that only meant the treasure was worth it, possibly bigger and better than she'd ever dreamed.

As CJ hung from her rope, trying to figure out what to do next, she held a single image in her mind. It was of her, standing at the wheel of a great pirate ship, the sea air in her face, the black skull-and-bones flag flapping in the breeze, and nothing but open waters ahead of her.

That was what she'd wanted since she was a little girl, and whatever was in that chest could buy it for her.

She racked her brain until she came up with a plan. Careful not to make too much noise, CJ reached down, grabbed a handful of rope, wound it three times around her left leg, and tied the end in a knot.

Then she held her breath and let go, tipping forward and landing upside down with a rough jerk that nearly made her grunt aloud. Hanging by only one leg, she gently swung herself toward the treasure chest, her hands just barely managing to snag the edge and stop her momentum.

Her next step was to open the chest. She knew there was no way she was going to be able to carry that giant box back up with her. She was a good rope climber, but she wasn't Gaston. So first she needed to know how much loot she was dealing with. Her plan was to fashion her pirate coat into a sack that she could tie around her waist, and then pull herself—and the treasure—back up the rope.

She felt around the edge of the chest for the clasp and tried to wrench it open, but it seemed to be stuck. She jiggled it, holding her breath as she listened for movement beneath her. All she needed right then was for one of those crocs to wake up and see her dangling in front of him like lunch on a stick.

Or a rope, rather.

All was quiet.

She tried the latch again, coming to the discouraging conclusion that it must be locked.

"Blast!" CJ cursed quietly, punching the air. She'd come all that way just to hit a dead end *there*? While she was hanging upside down in a crocodile pit?

Once again, CJ considered giving up and leaving. She was tired. She was dirty. She was dizzy from all the blood rushing to her head.

But something happened as she was dangling upside down. She felt something cold and hard shift beneath her ruffled pirate shirt. Her hands immediately moved to her collarbone, and that was when she remembered what she had tied there.

The *key*.

She scrambled to pull the string over her head and quietly felt around in the near pitch-darkness for the lock of the treasure chest.

The key fit perfectly. She turned it and heard a faint click. She could barely contain her excitement. It took every ounce of strength she had left not to rip open the lid and let all the beautiful jewels and gold coins gush out like a fountain. She had to be diligent, and quiet. She had to be careful not to wake those sleeping crocs.

So she held her breath and ever so slowly unlatched the clasp and eased open the lid. Her hands raced to catch the overflow of treasure before it clinked to the ground.

But nothing came out.

Confused, CJ lifted the lid the rest of the way, struggling to see inside the chest, but it was too dark. She fumbled in her pocket for another match and lit it, holding it above the open treasure chest. Inside was a thick swatch of velvety bloodred fabric with a single shiny object nestled in its folds.

What the . . . ?

But CJ barely had time to react, because at that very instant, she heard something move beneath her. She hastily glanced to her side and saw a single green eye illuminated by the tiny glow of her match.

Then someone—or some*thing*—let out a heavy breath and the flame went out.

ROPE'S END

It's been fun, but I think
I'll be going now.

CJ didn't have time to think.

She grabbed the object from the treasure chest, stuffed it into her pocket, and flung her self upward, grappling for the rope, just as she heard a set of teeth snap below her.

It was awake. And it was lunging for her.

And if one was awake, then soon they would all be awake.

With her heart thundering in her chest, she scrambled to untie her foot from the rope just as she heard another snap. She saw a glimmer of white teeth and felt a warm gust of air brush her fingertips.

Holy sea slugs, that was close.

CJ finally managed to untie the rope and pushed her feet against the side of the pit, swinging out of the way just as a dark shape leapt up and clamped its jaws shut.

The sound sent a chill down her spine.

CJ could have sworn the crocodile had missed completely, but then she felt the rope start to give way above her. She reached up and felt the rapidly unraveling strands. The crocodile had bitten through the rope.

She was hanging by a thread.

Below her, the crocs were stirring as more of them woke up to see what all the commotion was about.

She ran her hand against the cavern wall, searching for something to grab on to before the rope snapped completely, but there was nothing. Her nails scratched uselessly against the stone walls.

She heard a soft *Pop! Pop! Pop!* as the final strands of the rope unraveled. She shot her legs out to the sides in a split and just managed to wedge herself between the walls of the cave.

"Ow!" she cried as her leg muscles stretched farther than they'd ever stretched before. "That hurts!"

She felt another whoosh of air below her as one of the crocs snapped its teeth at her. Once again, CJ grappled along the walls for a groove or a notch, something she could use to pull herself up, but the stone was too smooth. If only she had something sharp she could spike into the stone. Something like a sword or a dagger or a . . .

Hook!

She reached into her pocket and felt the cool, sharp steel against her fingertips. Somehow the hook had not fallen out while she was hanging upside down. She grabbed the handle with her left hand and stabbed the sharp end as hard as she could into the wall above her head. It seemed to hold.

Using the hook to support her weight, she inched her split legs up along the walls. Then, making sure her feet were wedged safely in place, she disengaged the hook and thrust it back into the rock farther up.

As the crocodiles continued to lunge at her from below, making their frustration known with angry growls and bitter snaps of their teeth, CJ inched her way up the walls of the pit, until she finally reached the part of the rope that was still attached. She desperately grabbed it and climbed the rest of the way up.

When she emerged from the pit, she collapsed into a panting heap on the ground. She lay there for a good five minutes, struggling to catch her breath and calm her pounding heart. Far below she could still hear the crocodiles, outraged that they had missed out on their meal.

She leaned over the edge of the pit. "Sorry to disappoint you, guys," she taunted in a playful voice. Then she paused and added with a laugh, "No, I'm not."

THAR SHE BLOWS!

*Turns out sidekicks are sort
of useful-you know, when
they're not named Smee.*

It didn't take long for CJ to realize where she was. She was standing deep inside the right eye socket of the skull. She peered down into the great chamber below, where she and Freddie had rowed in on the boat. But the boat was nowhere to be seen.

"Freddie!" she called out. But only her own voice came back to her.

She tried again. *"Freddie!"*

There was still no answer. Where could she have

gone? Had she gotten washed out with the tide? But that didn't make sense. The tide was higher than ever now.

Then, a moment later, she heard Freddie's voice: "What are you doing over there?"

CJ glanced down and to her right. Freddie was still waiting under the *other* skull eye, where CJ had first climbed up the rock ladder. CJ searched frantically for a ladder on her side, but the stones beneath her were flat and slick.

She had two choices: to swing back across those hooks or to dive into the water.

Both options made her heart skitter.

When she looked down again, Freddie was already rowing the boat toward her. "Jump!" she called out to CJ.

CJ's whole body was seized by fear. Even though the tide had risen, making it a shorter drop, the idea of plunging into that water when she didn't know how to swim was paralyzing.

"I can't!" she shouted to Freddie.

"Yes, you can!" Freddie shouted back. "I'll be right here with the boat to get you."

CJ peered down again into the water.

"C'mon," Freddie coaxed her. "I won't let you drown."

CJ held her breath, closed her eyes, and leapt.

A moment later she felt the sting of the ice-cold water hit her everywhere. She started to flail, just like she had in the Enchanted Lake. But this time, when she tried to put her feet down, there was no floor. The water was too deep, and she started to sink, her heavy pirate coat weighing her down.

She opened her mouth to cry for help, but the sound never came out, because just then she felt herself being tugged upward. Freddie let out a grunt as she pulled CJ into the boat, collapsing breathlessly onto the bench.

Then Freddie looked at CJ and screamed.

CJ felt somewhat offended by the reaction. She knew she must look pretty shredded up from her hook-swinging and dallying with crocodiles and high-diving into the water, but she couldn't have looked *that* bad.

"What's happened to your hand?" Freddie cried, her voice shaking as she glared at CJ's left wrist.

That was when CJ realized she was still holding the hook. She laughed and dropped it to the ground, revealing her hand hidden beneath her sleeve.

Freddie clutched her chest. "Oh, thank the swampy bayou! I thought you'd *really* taken after your father."

CJ grimaced at the memory of all those crocodiles snapping and biting at her. "I nearly did."

Freddie looked her up and down, her face falling into a disappointed frown. "No treasure?" she asked.

"Actually," CJ said, "there was."

She reached into her coat pocket and pulled out the object she'd found inside the treasure chest.

It was a gold compass—her father's gold compass. The one that had been confiscated the day he was sent to the Isle of the Lost.

CJ had known it had to be his the moment she'd opened the chest—not because she'd ever seen it before, but because her father had described it so many times in such great detail. The solid-gold construction. The single flawless diamond set in the center. The swirling design etched around the border.

It was the very same one.

Freddie frowned at it. "That's it? We came all this way for *that*?"

CJ laughed. She'd had the very same reaction when she first saw it lying inside the chest. But now that she'd had some time to think about it, she realized that even though it might not have been the treasure of her dreams and the chest might not have been overflowing with precious jewels and coins of solid gold, somehow this was better.

When her father's compass had been taken away, it was as though his pirate spirit had been taken away. That compass was his guide, his token, his symbol of power.

And now it belonged to CJ.

"You don't understand," CJ told Freddie. "A compass is a pirate's source of information, her way of navigating through the world. Sure, it's not Mal's spell book, or Evie's magic mirror, or your shadow cards, but it's what I've got."

"It's also probably worth a fortune," Freddie said, taking it from CJ's hand and running her fingers over the smooth edges. "I mean, this looks like solid gold."

"Yeah," CJ replied somewhat absentmindedly. "And the diamond is as pure as they come. If I sold it, it would be more than enough to buy me a ship."

"So?" Freddie prompted her. "Are you going to sell it?"

CJ shrugged. "I don't know."

CJ had always believed that it was the ship that made the pirate. That was what she'd been basing her entire life plan on.

But what if it was something else? Something smaller?

Something like this?

Freddie turned the compass over in her hand, her eyes widening. "Look!" she exclaimed, holding it out for CJ to see.

CJ leaned in and stared, openmouthed, at the back of her father's most valuable possession. She hadn't even noticed it before, but there, engraved in the gold, were three letters:

CJH

"Captain James Hook," CJ said aloud.

"Hmmm." Freddie pondered. "I don't think that's what it stands for."

CJ shot her an impatient look. "Of course that's what it stands for. What else could it stand for? It was my *father's* compass."

"Not anymore," Freddie said, her eyes twinkling.

CJ took the compass and held it in her palm, staring at the letters again.

CJH.

Captain James Hook.

Or, she thought suddenly as a shiver ran down her arms, *CJ Hook.*

FAREWELL, MATEY!

So long, buckaroos.

*It's time for Freddie to drop anchor
and for me to set sail.*

CJ had spent so many hours sneaking around the campus of Auradon Prep she probably knew it better than the Fairy Godmother herself. Or at least she knew all the best places to hide there.

That was why sneaking back into the school was a breeze. CJ and Freddie rowed back to the bayou, stuffed their faces with one last plate of sugary beignets, and hitched a ride on another delivery truck bound for Auradon City. Then they waited until the sun had set and the students had all retired to their rooms before they crept across the campus and crawled through the first-floor window of Freddie's dorm room.

They both landed ungracefully in a heap on the floor.

"Ow!" Freddie cried. "Get your elbow off my hand!"

"Get your hand off my face!" CJ cried back.

"My hand isn't on your face!" Freddie replied. "That's my foot."

After they'd disentangled themselves and brushed the dirt from their already filthy outfits, they stood up and found they were not, in fact, alone.

Mal and Evie stood in the room, glaring at them with their arms crossed.

"Heeey, guys!" Freddie said, trying to sound innocent. "What's up? How's it going? So nice of you to wait up for us, but I am *sooo* tired." She fake yawned. "So if we could just chat tomorrow . . ."

The two VKs didn't move.

"We know you left the school without permission," Mal said, taking a step forward. "Audrey's been telling everyone she saw you in Briar's Hollow."

CJ saw the panic that flashed over Freddie's face. "Is Fairy Godmother going to expel me?"

Mal opened her mouth to say something, but CJ

180

stepped in. "It was my fault. Freddie didn't do anything wrong. I . . . I . . ." she stammered, searching for a good excuse that would clear her friend of any trouble. "I kidnapped her."

"You what?" Evie asked, perking up.

"I kidnapped her," CJ repeated, sounding more confident in her lie the second time. "I took her hostage. Family habits die hard."

"Is that true?" Mal asked Freddie.

Freddie glanced at CJ, who shot her a warning look. "Yes," Freddie finally replied. "She did. I told her I didn't want to leave. I didn't want to break the rules. But she . . . she . . ."

"I tied her up," CJ finished, sensing her friend was struggling to keep up the charade, "*and* taped her mouth shut. The whole pirate kit and caboodle. It was a hoot."

"No wonder your hair looks so horrendous!" Evie cried. She ran to Freddie and tried to fix her hair, but Freddie groaned and moved out of reach.

Mal, on the other hand, was much less quick to buy their story.

CJ watched Mal's reaction carefully. It was easy to fool the AKs—and apparently Evie, as well—but Mal was a different story. Back on the Isle of the Lost, she was pretty much the queen trickster. She could sniff out a lie just as easily as CJ could.

Mal stared at CJ like she was trying to shake her down with just a look.

She finally spoke. "I don't trust you, CJ."

"Aww. Thanks!" CJ said, flattered. "That's the nicest thing you've ever said to me, Malsy."

The scowl on Mal's face never faltered. "I don't know what you've been up to, but I really hope you're not planning on sticking around here."

CJ feigned disappointment. "Unfortunately, I can't. I have other plans. I was just stopping by to return my little hostage here." CJ patted Freddie's hair.

"Why is everyone trying to touch my head?" Freddie asked, moving away again.

CJ flashed Mal a cunning smile. "Will you be a dear and tell Fairy Godmother I'm sorry for taking one of her students hostage? And also make sure she doesn't expel our little friend? Especially since she had nothing to do with it. That would be extremely *un*–fairy godmother of her."

Mal opened her mouth to say something, but she never got the chance.

"Thanks!" CJ cooed in an overly bubbly voice.

"You're the worstest!" She looked from Mal to Evie and finally to Freddie. "Well, I'd love to stay and enjoy this slumber party—I'm sure you'll all have a jolly good time braiding each other's hair and talking about cute boys—but I have to run."

CJ turned and headed back to the window, stopping long enough to wave and call out, "Toodles!" before slipping into the night.

She smiled to herself as she strolled casually away from the building. But she didn't make it far before she heard someone hiss, *"Psst!"* behind her.

CJ turned to see Freddie's face in the dorm room window. She hurried back.

"Thanks for doing that," Freddie said, "for covering for me."

"Hey," CJ said with a coy wink, "what are partners for?"

CJ reached into her pocket and pulled out the matchbook Freddie had given her at Skull Rock, the one with the logo for the Bass Notes and Beignets jazz club on the front. "Thanks again for saving me." She tossed the matches to Freddie, who caught them adeptly with one hand. "I expect to see *you* on that stage next time I'm in the bayou."

Freddie grinned. "Are you sure you don't want to stay? I bet we could convince King Ben to let you enroll. He is a bit of a pushover."

CJ laughed. "Thanks, but I don't think I'm really cut out for the whole prep school life. Too many rules."

She dug her hand into the other pocket of her coat and ran her fingers over the compass—her *treasure*. It was heavy and solid and certain. It felt like a promise of something—something she'd dreamed about since she was a little girl: a journey she had a feeling was just beginning.

"Besides," she said to Freddie, squeezing the gold token that would be the key to her future one way or another, "my next adventure awaits me."

Then, with a mischievous smile, CJ turned and sailed off into the unknown.

Just before she rounded the corner, she heard Freddie whisper, "And so does mine."